Second Chance

Jill Debra Green

LIGHTHOUSE
BOOK PUBLISHING

© Jill Green 2020

Lighthouse Book Publishing
12 Dukes Court, Bognor Road
Chichester . PO19 8FX . United Kingdom
www.lighthousebookpublishing.com

ISBN: 978-1-9108483-9-5

You can contact the author via email using: jdg100@outlook.com ; www. jilldebragreen.com

Typesetting by Lighthouse Book Publishing
Cover Design by Sofia Froud
Printed and bound in the UK

One

The early rain had cleared, and although the threat of rain hung heavy in the air, pale bands of sunlight stretched through solid clouds and spattered on to the still-damp scene below. The huge rugby club grounds had become a bustling market this Tuesday morning. From very early morning traders had been arriving, their trailers stuffed and bulging with antiques, curios and collectables. By mid-morning most serious buyers had come and gone. The crowds had thinned, leaving the usual amateur enthusiasts and day trippers.

Catherine, in a pulled down beret and drab grey mac, dithered and hesitated over each tray of tat and treasure laid out for sale. Meandering through the alleys marked out by the stalls, every so often she would stand on tip-toe, crane her neck and look into the distance. Unsuccessful in her quest, she would return to her haphazard exploration, the whisper of a smile on her face. Fascinated by everything she saw, overwhelmed by the sheer volume and diversity of choice, she found herself unable to choose even one thing to buy. Catherine lingered at a horseshoe shaped stall draped in deep blue velvet cloth. Its hoard of precious little collectables was strewn across it like just-wet shells at the sea's edge, every piece a part of someone's history, now laid out for inspection and purchase. No longer special, but a commodity to be bargained for, and sold on at an even higher price. Catherine felt a moment's sorrow for all the Mauds, Alices and Ethels whose hatpins had finished up on a trader's table.

Amid all the sparkling glass and delicate china, there sat a squat little Toby Jug. It looked out of place. Catherine loved it immediately. Bravely, she reached out and picked it up. It depicted, surprisingly, a woman. A 'no-nonsense' figure, dressed in brown, sporting a blue shawl and jaunty tricorn hat. The jug was unexpectedly heavy and appeared to have suffered little damage from the passing years. She thought it must be a copy of a much older piece. It belonged on a heavy mantel piece above some farmers range, or to hang from a wooden beam in an old country pub. Catherine turned the jug in her hand, admiring the gingerbread glaze, the solid, compact design. She caught the eye of the stallholder, who was watching her suspiciously. Catherine put the little pot down quickly. Embarrassed, she spoke without intending to.

"Er…excuse me…how much for…the…er… the…sorry…how much would this be?"

The purveyor of fine antiques and collectables looked up with a 'you can't afford it' smile.

"That's fifty, dear," she drawled. "It's a very fine piece."

"Pence?" asked Catherine, before she could stop herself. The purveyor laughed indulgently. Catherine laughed, too loud. High pitched, almost hysterical.

"Yes, it is pretty," she squeaked. "I'll take it."

Catherine slipped the Toby jug into her bag. She didn't need it and had not intended to buy it. Graham, her husband, hated 'odds and ends' about the house. He would be sure to grumble at her. She cursed herself for being so weak, first for buying something she liked but Graham would not, and then for minding so much. She comforted herself that the little vase would at least have a good home and be valued for itself, not its price tag. She looked about her; there was still no sign of Bee, her friend, who had got lost somewhere between the ladies' toilet and the reclaimed architecture.

While Catherine's concern grew at having lost Bee, the lady herself was oblivious to the fact that Catherine was no longer with her. She finally noticed when, having bargained five pounds off a hideously overpriced glass bowl, she turned with a self-satisfied smirk to Catherine. When Catherine was not there, Bee, far from being worried, continued to shop as usual, cruising along each aisle, making eye contact with every stallholder. Hoping to intimidate or flirt the price down on every item. Bee had decided to fill her home with objects of value. She had been buying and studying all the right magazines for months. She knew exactly the style, the 'look' she wanted in her large mock Tudor home. The walls were daubed and papered in all the latest shades and techniques. The drapes were hung on the requisite hand-crafted iron poles, the rugs fashionably worn, the floor distressed. All it needed now was 'character' in the shape of a host of knick-knacks and curiosities, to be heaped about the place with 'style'. What most people accumulate over a lifetime through inheritance, good taste, or pure serendipity, Bee intended to purchase in a day. Since Catherine could offer neither advice nor approval, her absence was hardly noticed, let alone regretted.

Somewhere there was a mobile café. The smell of fried bacon snaked across the arena and pulled Catherine onwards. Over against a wall there nestled a gleaming, white caravan, with the words "MILADY'S SNACKS" emblazoned across the striped blind. A couple of plastic patio tables surrounded by chairs lay at each side of the serving hatch. In a moment of uncharacteristic decision, Catherine walked towards the snack bar intending to treat herself. She had not wanted to come to the market anyway, it had rained all the way here and Bee was lost without trace. On consideration, this last fact was actually an advantage, since Bee was a most embarrassing shopping companion. She imagined herself an expert on everything, which, when surrounded by true experts, was guaranteed to raise sardonic smiles or downright rudeness. Of course, Bee, living out her fantasy, was completely oblivious to their barely concealed mirth, or worse, contempt, but poor Catherine cringed on her friend's behalf.

The arrogantly unwitting source of this embarrassment had by now loaded herself up with various trinkets and bits. Finding it increasingly difficult to rummage through the various displays with a heavy bag on her shoulder, she finally decided that she needed Catherine to carry her bags. Muttering under her breath at the selfishness of her 'so-called friend', she set out to find her.

The last half hour had been a pleasant interlude in an otherwise dreadful day. Since they had become separated, Catherine had had the opportunity to look around alone and unremarked. Bee was sure to ferret her out soon, Catherine strode purposefully towards the counter and ordered a mug of tea. She stood at the counter.

"Anything else, dear?" asked 'Milady,' a short, square shaped woman in her late fifties, assisted by the ubiquitous, sullen, lank-haired teenager.

"Why not?" replied Catherine, resolutely. "A bacon sandwich, please."

"Brown or white, dear?" The woman slapped two plump rashers on the griddle.

"White, please, with Ketchup!" Catherine grinned brightly in anticipation.

The woman looked up, "A woman after my own heart," she declared to the entire world. "Go sit down dear, I'll bring it over."

Catherine sat on one of the plastic chairs. They made her think of Graham, her husband of more than twenty years. He had very fixed ideas on such things. "Plebs have plastic furniture on paving stone patios," he explained when she suggested they get some. "I think we can set our sights a little higher than that!"

'Plebs' loomed large in Graham's world. They were those who had not reached the dizzy heights of senior management, did not belong to the Golf club and could only look on in awed admiration as Graham piled achievement upon achievement and possession upon possession. Whether Catherine remained one of those prized acquisitions, or was, by now, relegated to awed bystander, she did not know. She felt she should be grateful that she was still there at all. He had a way of speaking that made her immediately feel foolish, stupid, yet resentful that he should do so. For years, he had systematically patronised, bullied and belittled her, so that she now found herself unable to make a decision or voice an opinion. She had been the grammar schoolgirl, bright, pretty and going places until she fell under the spell of Graham Chandler. Her parents had never liked him, which had only made her more determined to prove them wrong. Some months before her eighteenth birthday, she found herself pregnant and rushed from wedding day fantasy to marriage and motherhood.

Fate threw her in the deep end when she had twins, Simon and Helen. Reality dropped in like manure from a tipper-truck on the twin's first birthday. Having promised to join the little family party, Graham failed to arrive. Catherine phoned the office to be told that, "Mr Chandler had gone home at lunch time for his children's birthday." He then phoned her to say that he had piles of work, the manager would not hear of him leaving early. The party went ahead without him. That night, like some B-movie cliché, he came home late, smelling of whisky and another woman's perfume, reciting some tale of a quick drink after working late. She had hoped then that this would be the only time. She blamed herself, her preoccupation with the twins, her baby fat. Yet despite her efforts to regain a foothold in his life, nothing changed. The affairs continued, more or less discreetly, and Catherine continued to pretend it didn't hurt at all. She finally understood this was how it would always be. She told herself she was resigned to it, but had lately begun to realise that she just could not be bothered to object.

"Round of bacon & ketchup and a nice mug of tea!" Catherine jumped involuntarily as the little feast thumped down onto the table in front of her.

"Sorry," she said, "I was miles away!"

"No need to apologise dear!" The woman had brought two mugs of tea. "Mind if I join you? It's gone quiet for a minute. Kelly can shout if there's a sudden rush!" Catherine motioned her to sit, surprised at her familiarity, but pleased to be asked. Easing herself onto the seat, 'Milady' asked Catherine if she was in the antiques trade.

Catherine laughed. "Not at all," she replied, "I didn't even want to come. I was coerced! Bee, the neighbour I came with, is rather hard to refuse. She thinks she's going to find a long-lost Gainsborough or something. I'm just the driver." She sighed.

Milady cocked her head to one side. "Don't you like this sort of thing, then?"

"I don't really know much about it," She replied. "I love to see all these beautiful things; I only wish I knew enough to appreciate them properly. It's the 'cash n wrap' attitude to it all that disturbs me. People seem to be looking for profit not pleasure."

"They've all got a living to make, and most dealers start out as collectors," Milady replied, "But I must agree it looks like a feeding frenzy here at the start." Catherine laughed as the woman continued, "It's the thrill of the hunt, buying something for a fiver, that you know you can sell for ten pounds, finding something unusual, special. They're all collectors at heart, you know."

"Sounds like you are, too."

"I must confess that the bug has bitten me too. I have a few things passed down through the family and I add to them when I can. It's very tempting, going to these fairs every week. You'll be hooked as well once you get started!" warned 'Milady,' jovially.

Catherine laughed, "I can believe it! I could have spent a fortune this morning, it's fascinating!" She had dreaded coming to what she pictured as a noisy crowded little hall, full of dusty, dog-eared relics and shark like dealers. Instead, she found a vast maze both indoors and out, stuffed full and fascinating. In fact, rather than resenting Bee's insistence on the visit, Catherine found that she was rather enjoying herself; particularly since Bee had disappeared. The conversation continued.

"In spite of myself," Catherine remarked, "I really am rather pleased I came."

"Glad to hear it. Let me introduce myself, I'm Florence Starling, my friends call me Floss." Catherine shook her hand and introduced herself in return.

Floss was not Catherine's idea of a typical snack bar owner. Although she looked the part, being rosy cheeked, rounded and sunny, she spoke in what could only be described as 'upper class' tones. She wore a huge red felt hat which entirely covered her hair, Catherine later discovered this to be a very effective way to keep out the smell of fried food. Floss pulled a half-packet of biscuits from the marsupial pouch of her apron; they had been sealed by twisting the empty top of the pack, which she now unsealed by holding the twist and rotating it. The contents burst out, shooting butter crunch creams across the table. Both Catherine and Floss swatted the biscuits one by one to prevent them falling onto the wet, grimy tarmac beneath. When the safety of each biscuit was ensured they both sat back, laughing.

"Well, looks like we're both top of the league at biscuit catching!" Floss grinned, dunking her biscuit into her tea.

The two women sized each other up in a quick glance. Floss saw a youngish woman dressed older than her years. An open, honest face which was really quite pretty, if you could look through the worried half frown, and past the dreadful pull-on fluffy hat, and shapeless old Mac. Catherine saw a woman in her late fifties, confident, open and cheerful. The huge red hat clashed wildly with her brightly patterned tunic and tie-dyed trousers. Floss pulled off the hat to reveal a froth of red curls with the occasional glint of silver, she caught Catherine's eye. "Do you like it?" she grinned, adjusting the collar of her tropical trouser suit. It's Indonesian."

Catherine hesitated. "It's very striking" she replied, diplomatically.

Floss laughed some more. "Loud, some might say! I love bright colours. Customers like to see someone cheerful when they hand over their money, a splash of colour's good for business!"

Catherine thought it was a bucketful rather than a splash, but had to admit that Floss' personality was most definitely expressed in the clothes she wore. And Floss, had it occurred to her to do so, could have said the same for Catherine. Leaning forward, Catherine smiled as if imparting a secret.

"I love the way you dress," she said, "but my husband has very particular ideas on fashion. I've rather given up the fight, and besides, dark colours hide the bulges!" Seeing Flosses enquiring expression, Catherine tried to explain. "He thinks the wife of a man in his position should dress 'appropriately'. He's a sales director; he likes things done his way." She looked sad, not bitter.

Floss saw the regret in her eyes, or was it despair? Catherine saw the flash of unasked for sympathy. She scrabbled to his defence. "It's his reputation with the company...image, you know...anyway, I don't know why I'm saying all this," she finished weakly.

"My dear!" I know just what you're saying," Floss replied, all too brightly. The casual conversation was taking a strange turn, her heart went out to this unhappy woman, and she *was* unhappy, whether she realised it or not. "I conformed to all that for years, but it's my turn now, and they can all think what they want. It used to be called doing your own thing, I believe!"

Catherine looked genuinely surprised at this daring statement. "Don't you care then?"

"Used to, but not anymore. My husband died a few years back and I realised I had spent so much time worrying about what I wasn't, that I had forgotten who I really was." Catherine began to make sympathetic noises; Floss shushed her. "Don't worry about all that" she laughed. "I'm as over it as I will ever be now. Don't mistake me, I still miss dear Harry, but if he were here now, I would not be trundling around the country selling fry-ups from a van. Harry would have disapproved terribly." She sighed. "That sounds terrible doesn't it? Not very emancipated at all!"

Catherine smiled "Well, it depends on your point of view; some people would say that marriage and emancipation are mutually exclusive!"

"In some cases, they'd be right!"

"I suppose most of us make the best of things"

The conversation was becoming uncomfortable. Catherine found it easy to talk to this stranger, but she felt she was saying too much. Floss sensed this drawing back and brought them on to safe ground again. Small talk was Catherine's strong point. They chatted for a few minutes about the weather, the business of the market, the suitability of the venue and so on. Catherine mentioned her children and naturally, asked Floss about hers.

"We were never blessed with them, sadly; although when Harry's widowed mother died his younger brother, Andrew, came to live with us. He was

14

twelve and very angry, we'd only been married a couple of years. It was a terrible time, losing a parent, gaining a reluctant son, and trying to keep body and soul together at the same time."

Catherine grimaced sympathetically, "Sometimes a crisis brings people closer together."

"Precisely," nodded Floss. "We had our difficulties, everyone does." Catherine nodded in agreement. "But we all survived. Harry and I were very happy together, and when he died suddenly from a heart attack three years ago, Andrew was a tower of strength. I was in a daze for months until..."

A sudden clattering of heels and Catherine felt her shoulder clamped by a bony hand. "There you are, Catherine," a pretentiously loud voice boomed. "*Where* in God's name have you been?" It was Bee, dressed in her 'shrewd dealer' outfit of leather trousers, faux-fur jacket and numerous gold chains; it seemed they were now to be loudly re-united.

Catherine apologised breathily, she hated scenes. "I thought I'd sit tight until you appeared," she added, laughing nervously. She squirmed an apologetic, hopeless smile at Floss.

Bee gave Floss a 'you may go' face, saying to Catherine, "Well, while you were sitting stuffing yourself in a greasy spoon, I was going frantic. I know you didn't want to come. I wouldn't put it past you to go home without me."

Catherine flinched. "Bee, that's not fair, you know I wouldn't do that!"

Embarrassed on Catherine's behalf, Floss rose to go, wiping the table as she did. "Well, customers waiting," she chirped. "Time to go. I enjoyed talking with you Catherine."

Bee glared at Catherine. "First name terms with the caterer, eh?" She jeered, just loud enough for Floss to hear and, Bee hoped, feel put in her place. "We *are* going up in the world." Bee laughed, "I thought I'd find you near the food!"

Catherine rose from her seat, resigned to Bee's malicious banter. Bee would continue to vent her spleen in the usual vicious monotone until she felt Catherine had learned her lesson. Catherine trailed obediently after her. She tried to respond. "Actually, she was very interesting to talk to, I liked her."

"Trying to cultivate a good customer, no doubt," sniffed Bee, looking Catherine up and down, then strode off briskly towards the indoor stalls.

Catherine followed, turning to wave apologetically at Floss, who, with raised eyebrows and a wry smile, returned her wave. They were an odd pair, Floss thought, Catherine, plain and dowdy apologising at every breath, with her brash shopping partner, Bee, all false tan, false nails and highlights. "Takes all sorts," she muttered, turning to serve the next hungry customer.

Sometime later, the promised rain returned. Having trailed around the remaining stalls behind a loudly inexpert Bee, Catherine suggested they return to the car. Bee did not argue, since her artificially straight hair would not stand up to prolonged exposure to nature, and the two were soon cruising through the suburban countryside. Bee was overflowing with self-congratulation at the many bargains she had wrenched from the reluctant dealers, who, she implied, were helpless in the face of her fearsome expertise, beauty and business acumen. Her incessant babble became wallpaper to the rooms in Catherine's imagination; rooms where Bee took her newly acquired hoard to a televised antique show; where the TV expert, on seeing Bee's 'little something I picked up at Shore Park' would scream with laughter and cry, "They saw you coming!" Public humiliation in front of fifty million viewers. Very satisfying. She became aware of silence.

"*Well*... are you listening?"

Catherine sighed. "Sorry," she replied, "I was concentrating. The weather's getting worse."

"Honestly, Catherine, *you're* getting worse." Bee grumbled. "I asked if you bought anything, or was it a complete waste of time taking you?"

"Oh, I enjoyed pottering about looking at all the bits and pieces..."

"Bits and pieces!" interrupted Bee, "fine antiques and collectibles are hardly that. Really, you're such a pleb, it's a good thing you've got me to show you the finer things in life!"

She said it as a joke, but Catherine knew that Bee really felt she was educating her. In order for it to be so, Catherine submitted, out of some perverse sense of politeness, to Bee's condescension. To cover her embarrassment, or sometimes even anger, Catherine would laugh her nervous, dry laugh. This only served to confirm Bee's self-image of the sophisticated woman with an adoring bumpkin for a friend. Catherine laughed, but really did feel angry. Bee laughed and felt triumphant. Glancing across at her plump friend, Bee congratulated herself on having found a plain, fat friend who could drive. It was so convenient and meant that whenever they were out together, she was sure of getting the most attention; Bee, supremely confident, abysmally shallow.

The conversation wound through the usual subjects, like landmarks on a familiar road, husband's careers, the golf club, Bee's gym, Bee's favourite TV programs. Bee chattered on and on. Driving home through the four o'clock traffic, Catherine watched as mothers and children scurried home from school. It seemed so long ago and yet only yesterday that she was dragging Helen and Simon to and from school. The closeness and bustle of those primary school years was followed by the slow pulling apart, as the children gained independence and adulthood. Helen, always quick and brutally direct, had decided at the age of fourteen that hairdressers earned plenty of money. She got herself a Saturday job in 'Topknots' at the corner of the village, then sailed through her apprenticeship at a big salon in town, single-minded in her mission to be as independent as possible, as quickly as possible. Helen was now, at the age of 23, owner of a high-end salon in the Midlands. Catherine's daughter rarely came home, rarely phoned. When she did visit, Catherine felt it was more from duty than affection.

There had always been a sort of understanding between Helen and her father. 'Daddy's girl' he called her. But even that tie had become more fragile through the years. In Catherine's eyes they were so alike, Helen and Graham, both single minded, ambitious, self-absorbed. You could begin a conversation with either one of them and the talk would turn to centre on themselves. Graham would boast to anyone who would listen of his dynamic daughter, but their son, Simon, was hardly mentioned. If his name came up Graham would denounce him as a waster, a bleeding-heart.

Simon was working for a church community project in the North of England. Providing a café alongside clubs, activities, and support groups for everyone and anyone, the magnificent old church of St Christopher's had become as busy during the week as it ever had been on a Sunday. Simon's job was to run the centre, oversee the many volunteers and assist the

Minister in his mission to love every soul they encountered.

Graham and Helen would only act in their own interests; even favours or kindnesses were calculated to further their careers, or project the right image.

"That's why they are both successful people," Catherine told herself, but could not help thinking how much pain their success had caused her. Years of putting them first, listening to their plans and aspirations, swallowing up her own in the realisation of theirs. Years of bolstering their already swollen egos, years of releasing them from the mundane in their lives, had only served to diminish her in their eyes. Far from recognising and valuing her contribution, both Helen and her father treated Catherine with contempt.

Graham's ruthless ambition had given them a comfortable lifestyle. He had fought and fawned his way through various companies and positions and was now, as he was so fond of saying, a top man in a top job. Graham at twenty-eight had been a skilled seducer. He wore nothing but black and drove a red sports car, which gave him an air of dangerous chic. His interest in his very young wife was fed by her fascination with him. His determination to marry her had been a response to her parent's obvious disdain, rather than true feeling for her.

Very soon after their wedding day he had returned to his unmarried lifestyle. The secrecy only added to the excitement. The affairs continued and Graham emerged as the man that Catherine's parents always knew he was. Like one balloon filling from another, his pride and self-confidence inflated, while Catherine's became shrivelled and useless. She maintained the pretence of a happy marriage; her own pride would allow her to do no less, but she was making the best of a bad job.

When Catherine's mother died, her father, John, handed the keys of his family home to his daughter, and bought himself a pretty cottage within easy visiting distance. However, John had never been happy with Catherine's choice of husband, and the more he saw, the less he liked. He showed this disapproval in his will. Unknown to anyone but himself and Catherine, he had left the family home to his grandson Simon, on condition that it was a home to Catherine for her lifetime; thus ensuring that neither Graham nor Helen could ever get their hands on it.

Bee was still talking as the car pulled up outside her 1930s mock Tudor home, built well after Catherine's home, which stood opposite.

"Not too fast, Cath," she admonished, "it wrecks the gravel."

Catherine got out and opened the boot for Bee's precious parcels. As she turned to hand them over, Bee was already at the front door.

"Just put them *carefully* on the kitchen table, would you?" she commanded, pushing the door open and clattering off to the bathroom.

Catherine did as she was told. Looking up she saw the kitchen calendar scribbled through with various appointments. "ROGER HOME" was scrawled and underlined heavily in red.

Bee reappeared. "That's better," she sighed.

Catherine turned to her, "I couldn't help noticing Roger's home next Sunday. Holiday?"

"Oh, he's got a course in London on Monday, doesn't have to drive back to Head Office until Monday night."

"That'll be nice for you both," smiled Catherine, "an extra day together."

Bee huffed. "Very romantic," she drawled. "He'll just be in the way, I expect." Then bustling once more, "Sorry I can't offer you a coffee, must get on, you know how it is, busy, busy, busy!" She almost pushed Catherine out of the door.

Catherine returned to her car, reversed out of Bee's drive and then into her own, muttering in a high-pitched imitation of Bee's silly drawl, "Thanks *so much* for being my taxi and packhorse, *so sorry* you got soaked to the skin, thanks so very, *very,* much!"

*****

Catherine smiled as she parked the car in the garage and let herself into her own warm kitchen. As she made herself a cup of tea, she dialled her father's number.

"Hello Katie," he answered.

"How did you know it was me?"

"Caller ID. Don't you have it? I only have to answer the phone if I want to talk to the person on the other end!"

"Oh, Dad, you're not avoiding some amorous old duck again, are you?"

"The very idea!" he protested. "Anyway, what's new?"

"Well, I went to a huge antique fair today, with Bee."

John let out a derisory laugh.

"Oh Dad, she's not that bad!"

"She's no better than she should be, as your dear Mum would have said!" She could hear the smile in his voice. "Anyway, what did you get up to?"

"Actually, I managed to lose her. When I found her again, she was loaded with *priceless* antiques, which, of course, *I* carried to the car!"

Retired from his veterinary practice in the village, John now led a busy life, mostly centred on his Church, and was often heard to say that he wondered how he had ever had time to work. His frequent telephone chats with Catherine, his only child, were very important to him, and her visits were a pleasure to them both. John, a youthful man in his early sixties was a committed member of his local church and had sung in the choir since childhood. He loved walking his dog on the nearby common and was an avid reader of murder mysteries. Catherine's tales of her day with Bee was typical of his daughter's generosity of nature. John sometimes despaired at his daughter's yielding nature, but consoled himself with the thought that he really did have the most caring and thoughtful daughter a man could wish for.

They continued their easy chat; Catherine looked forward to tomorrow's coffee and Danish with him, their weekly 'date' when she dropped off his shopping and they exchanged conversation.

Two

Roger and Bee had been their friends since they had bought the house next door a few years ago. Bee and Graham, being the outgoing ones, had arranged barbecues, outings and suppers, which both Roger and Catherine had gone along with, rather than initiated. Through much primping, plumping and plastering, Bee looked much younger than Catherine, though she was in fact several years older. Roger was younger than them both.

From the outset, Bee had been aggressively ambitious for Roger. She had insisted they buy the right type of home in the 'better' part of town. She cultivated the right sort of friends, that is, those who could be useful to them, and encouraged him to do the same. She joined the gym, the golf club and the Church of England. Bee's entertainment budget was phenomenal, her parties legendary.

Still only in his mid-thirties, Roger had already become director of a large design company. All the verve and ability which had thrust him to the top of the corporate tree was drawn from the wellspring of Bee's ambition. His success was due largely to her single-mindedness. To many of his colleagues she epitomised the corporate wife. Hard, manipulative and predatory, she was simultaneously ridiculed and feared. Yet Bee's love for Roger was genuine, and his every promotion was her gift to him.

Essentially a gentle, creative man, leadership did not come easily to Roger. He was well aware that the credit, or was it blame, for his senior position in the rat-race was all Bee's. Initially attracted to Bee's strength of character, he saw in her the glamorous, supportive and dynamic partner he longed for. She had directed, organised, coddled and cajoled him for nearly ten years and he had submitted gladly. More recently, however, the late-maturing boy in him began to see the prize as dearly won.

To him, Bee's strength became domineering, her encouragement nagging, and her striving after his next goal mere vanity. When he looked in the mirror, Roger saw a prisoner. He found himself playing a walk-on role in Bee's determined life story. His personality had become a projection of her own; he was weary, disenchanted, and shame ridden for being so ungrateful.

Bee, on the other hand, had failed to see the relationship drifting through her fingers. She saw herself as she imagined other people saw her. In her mind she was the sophisticated, beautiful companion of an adoring, strikingly handsome and brilliant man. So cocooned was she in this fantasy world of her own making, she was blind to the truth. The gifted and once malleable young man had become quieter, almost withdrawn at times, yet she did not allow it to dent the steely façade she had worked so hard to build. If the hint of a suspicion should enter her mind to threaten her world, Bee put it in a box marked 'Don't Look!' and thereby dismissed it.

*****

Monday morning found Catherine filling bin liners and boxes with the contents of her loft. The local school was having its annual summer Fete and Jumble Sale and had left a leaflet asking for unwanted goods. Old books and vases, clothes now too small, even toys were all transferred from their long forgotten resting place to be collected and transported to the school hall that afternoon. The job was soon finished. Catherine amused herself with the thought that she was probably throwing out something highly collectable. It felt strange to her, who normally clung on to the past, to sweep away a quantity of the mementoes and remains of the last twenty years. Graham would be pleased; he hated her tendency to hoard. Sentimentality, he called it. Graham lived for today.

Catherine packed up the last box and piled the whole lot by the front door ready to be loaded on the van later. Graham and Roger were playing golf, as usual, and she was expected to 'shop and lunch' with Bee. Usually

Bee shopped, or rather flitted, from one stylish (or even style-less) department store to another, while her frumpy friend bobbed along behind as usual. Catherine's interest in clothes had never been great, and over the years had diminished even further. As long as it was presentable, and Graham did not disapprove, she was happy, unlike Bee, who had to have the latest hairstyle, the latest fashion however ridiculous it made her look. As for seeking Roger's approval, it never occurred to her to do so. Or that he should have anything but a good opinion of anything she chose to do.

The ladies shopped; the men played golf. Catherine and Bee returned and were seated at Catherine's big kitchen table, drinking tea. Catherine's feet hurt. Bee was droning on and on about her purchases. Catherine had become adept at nodding and making the right noises in the right places, her mind wandering as Bee held out for comment blouses, scarves, shoes, candles, earrings and the rest of her day's plunder. She thought about the antiques fair, meeting Floss, buying the sweet little Toby jug. Of course, Graham had scoffed in disgust when he saw it on the mantelpiece. He mocked and chided until she gave in and took it away. She put it on the kitchen windowsill. It made her smile. To him it may be ugly; to her it was full of character, dependable, special.

Graham would be home from his day's golf with Roger soon. As usual the Saturday ritual of golf for the men and day out for 'the girls' would be followed by a meal at the local restaurant for all of them. Catherine often wondered if the advantage of not having to cook really outweighed the disadvantage of spending the evening in such a predictable way. More often than not, however, it was a pleasant enough ending to the week. Roger and Catherine looking on as the other two discussed the latest 'must-have' gadget or accessory; or pulling apart the new neighbours' taste in garden ornaments. Graham would say, "More Aldi than 'arrods!" and they would all laugh along with it.

Bee was still talking when the front door opened abruptly. It was Graham. He swore as the door banged onto Catherine's boxes for the bazaar. Catherine called out a greeting to which there was no response except the sound of crashing china as he kicked the boxes out of his way. He had obviously had a bad day's golf. He shouted, "What is all this crap?" accompanied by more kicking and swearing.

"It's for the School Fete," Catherine replied nervously. "Sorry. You normally come in the back door."

"Well I didn't today, alright!" As he spoke, he poked his head around the kitchen door, his tone exaggeratedly patronising, his face covered in a sarcastic smile. His eyes fell on Bee. The change in manner was immediate. He crossed the floor to kiss her cheek.

"How's my sexy next-door neighbour?" he crooned intimately.

Bee gave Catherine an almost triumphant look. She returned the kiss.

"How's Grumpy Graham?" she smooched.

"Sorry about that, darling, your beloved husband was on a winning streak today. And didn't we know it!"

Catherine was apparently invisible as they talked about his bad luck at golf. Bee sympathised and pointed out that the last thing he needed was to walk into a pile of black sacks and white elephants after all his trouble. The conversation turned to Catherine's 'ways.' Bee regaled him with her tale of Catherine getting lost at the market. He responded with tales of her incompetence around the house and the 'ugly vase.' They reeled with laughter.

"She must have known how awful it was, she didn't even tell me she had bought it!" Bee howled.

Catherine laughed along with them, as she was expected to.

Graham feigned tragic surprise "What, you haven't seen this antique wonder! You don't know what you're missing! Go and get it Catherine."

"There's no need, really," Catherine ventured "It's nothing special."

Graham persisted, "Get it!" he spat through gritted teeth. "Give your friend a laugh."

Catherine blushed, her eyes filled with tears, she was humiliated, abused. Bee sensed that things had gone too far. She felt almost sorry for her unhappy friend.

"Don't get it for my sake," she touched Catherine's hand. "I have got to go. Roger will be waiting for me." She began to leave, turned as she opened the back door. "If the jug's that bad, stick it in the School Fete!" Both she and Graham guffawed at her wit. She mimed a cheery wave to Catherine, pecked Graham's cheek and left.

Catherine stood and busied herself with the tea cups. Catherine caught her reflection in the kettle as she refilled it; her face was bowed grotesquely, a likeable buffoon. She had come to expect their jokes and innuendoes; her apparent unconcern was a form of paralysis, brought about by constant adjustment and readjustment of her personality to conform to Graham's wishes. If, in company, a part of her true self emerged, he would slap it down again with a few well-chosen words. "Are you drunk?" he would ask. "You don't normally act like this!" Or, "Catherine, I'm sure our guests don't want to hear all this drivel." Then, to the world, "I don't know what's got into her!"

The doorbell rang. It was the man collecting for the school. He was very impressed with both the quality and the quantity of her contribution. She was happy to be thought well of by a complete stranger. How pathetic she had become! She returned to the kitchen to find Graham had made himself a coffee.

"Didn't make you one," he said "you stand chatting to these people for so long, it's a waste of time," She looked at him and saw the Toby Jug behind him. Hoping he wouldn't see it, she smiled at him. "What the hell's got into you?" he exclaimed, sarcastically.

"Nothing, really" she whispered.

"Oh, for God's sake, woman, speak up. Something's the matter. What am I supposed to do, beg you to tell me?"

The telephone rang; Catherine jumped. Graham turned and walked towards the stairs. Catherine picked up the receiver; it was her son.

"It's Simon," she called.

"Well, hallelujah and whoop-de-do," drawled Graham.

*****

Arriving back in her own home, Bee heard Roger talking. She shouted a hello. Roger appeared at the top of the stairs in his bathrobe, towel-drying his hair.

"Who was that?" she demanded.

"Who?"

"On the phone. You were on the phone."

"I was singing in the shower, Bee. No-one's on the phone."

She climbed the stairs to join him, her hands beginning to loosen his belt. He pulled away, retying the belt.

"Golf was hard work today. I'm worn out."

Bee sighed, disdainfully. "You're getting dull, Roger, dull, dull, dull."

She pushed past him into the bathroom and began to run a bath for herself, pouring in the chosen rejuvenating essences. It would take her all of the remaining two hours to prepare herself for the informal evening out.

Roger slumped on to the bed, staring into nowhere in particular. He was angry with Bee. He was angry with himself. He still cared for her, but he felt smothered. Did he love her? Probably not anymore. Had he ever loved her? He knew now that he never had. Did he like her? Not at all. He had been a shy young man with a genius for digital design and innovation, she had seen his potential and steered him from backroom anonymity into the uncomfortable glare of corporate partnership. Every day, the sheer effort of pretending to be 'like them' was draining his life away. The world she inhabited seemed pointless - a complex, counterfeit realm where nobody said what they really meant and everyone else understood the hidden agenda. Bee irritated him, every word and gesture seemed to add to his distaste for her company. Roger knew that he owed all he had to Bee's assiduous work on his behalf and it was only a kind of grateful guilt that kept him at her side. Looking at himself in the mirror, he saw a man who hadn't changed much on the outside. A few lines about the eyes, and how tired those eyes looked. Tired of the routine life had become. Tired of the overwhelming effort needed to conform daily to everyone else's expectations. Tired of playing those grown-up games of success, one-upmanship, relationships.

His mobile phone rang from the pocket of his suit Jacket, flung over the back of the chair. He grabbed it quickly, speaking in a hushed voice.

"Hi, you…Yes…Sorry. She walked in. I had to hang up…She's in the bath now…No, it's OK. I can talk for a minute."

He stood and pushed the door shut. Hanging on the back of the door, as usual, were the clothes Bee had chosen for him to wear that night.

"She'll be in there for ages; the meal's booked for 7:30, only two hours to spare…I'm just getting dressed."

The caller made some sharp comment and they both laughed. He began to remove the outfit, charcoal trousers and pale grey checked shirt, from its hanger. She had even laid his underwear out on the bed. The conversation continued in low, intimate tones. He described the clothes he was about to put on.

"You know I'm not bothered," he sighed. "She likes me to look the part, I suppose…no, not a nerd"

"…I can't wear that," he whispered, smiling. "She hates it…"

"…Well, just for you, but you realise my life will be hell all evening."

The lady at the other end of the line seemed to propose some incentive for undergoing such torture. More sweet talk, promises and forecasts of doom ensued, interlaced with soft laughter. Roger's face was alive, alight with the joy of a well-kept secret.

"Okay, okay," he said, "I give in, but there'll be hell to pay!"

The clothes Bee had chosen for him were returned to the wardrobe. Roger replaced them with a much younger looking fashionable outfit which had been squashed to the back. As he dressed, he and his lover exchanged the tender endearments of a hidden affair.

*****

Catherine and Graham were arguing. Well, as near as Catherine dared to get to disagreeing with Graham and as far as Graham would allow her to. Catherine was hurt at Graham's treatment of their son, amazed that he would not even come to the phone. During her conversation with Simon, Graham had, as usual, shouted various obscenities and sarcasms as she remarked on each piece of news. Catherine liked to hear Simon's enthusiasm for the work he did. Unlike Graham, who felt that Simon's education was wasted on these 'down and outs.'

Catherine was proud of her son. She was proud that the boy she had brought up to be caring and responsible, had grown into a man with just those qualities. She was proud that her own son was making a real difference to real people. She was proud that Simon's success could be counted in lives changed for the good. His whole attitude was 'what can I do for you?' rather than Graham's 'what can you do for me?'

Graham could not, or would not see her point of view. Her caring son was, to him, a bleeding-heart do-gooder, and his faith religious mania. Graham had been a strict father to Simon, bombarding him constantly with 'rules for life,' upbraiding him for every little misdemeanour, from using the wrong knife to speaking too fast. Simon would bring home an excellent school report, only to be told it was no more than should be expected. Having sent Simon to a fee-paying church school, Graham was horrified to learn that his son was becoming attracted to the religious as well as the academic aspect of his education. Graham would deride, belittle and threaten Simons' interest in the Christian faith, having no doubt his son would see sense and give it up in favour of more realistic ambition. Untiringly kind, respectful and dutiful towards Graham, Simon's insistence on following this faith was unshakeable.

Simon, from the start of his second term at University, had begun to work for 'St Christopher's Mission,' a charity set up to bring practical help, encouragement and spiritual renewal to the most run-down parts of the country. Graham all but stopped talking to him.

Simon had been with St Christopher's for over three years now, and Catherine had noticed that one name in particular had begun to crop up more and more often in Simon's telephone conversation. Laura, a volunteer, seemed to spend a lot of time with Simon. Whenever Simon described a situation or regaled his mother with the latest amusing anecdote, Laura was in there somewhere. Maybe there was something in it, Catherine hoped.

Simon heard his father's customary mocking comments, but this time, unexpectedly, his mother made no attempt to excuse them.

*****

Bee, meanwhile, had left the steaming bathroom and was blow drying and styling her hair at the bedroom mirror. Her roots needed doing. She was glad her next appointment was only a few days away. She inspected her acrylic nails. Maybe a manicure, too. The heated rollers were ready; she put a few in the front of her hair, then began the long, precise, and pleasurable process of applying her evening make-up. She had just finished applying the final strokes of lipstick, when Roger shouted up the stairs, reminding her of the time. Bee swore. She was worth waiting for, she thought, worth every minute. She dressed in a low-cut, short-skirted dress and floated downstairs.

"At last," grumbled Roger, standing.

She stood at the doorway, pouting. "How do I look?" She skipped across the room, arms outstretched turning slowly for approval, finishing up with a girlish wiggle.

"Fine," he replied, shortly. "Now can we go? The others will have finished the first course by now."

Bee was incensed. She had expected warm and overt appreciation. Instead there was a cold rebuke. Roger could see her hurt. He tried to recover.

"Sorry, sweetheart, you look great, really. You know I hate to be late."

"Don't make me laugh!" Bee rounded on him. "You were late for everything until you met me." She looked him up and down and snarled "What the hell are you wearing?"

"You've seen it before," he protested. "Don't act so surprised."

"Seen it and hated it," she spat. "You never could choose your own clothes. I don't know what made you think you could. Next time you're on a business trip, buy yourself a watch or something. You look ridiculous!"

"I like it," was Roger's only response to her vitriol. He could have said that she looked ridiculous too, in her teenager's clothes. Grotesque, foolish, pathetic.

"Don't cross me, Roger," she hissed. "You'll regret it."

He looked, without expression, into her eyes, thinking, 'I don't love you,' but saying, "Let's go."

*****

They arrived at the restaurant to find Graham and Catherine had ordered the first round of drinks. Graham, as usual, had to make his comparison between Bee in her skimpy, sexy dress, and Catherine in her demure black twinset, pearls and corduroy skirt. Bee basked in his admiration. Roger took his seat in silence, nodded tersely at Catherine and deliberately excluded himself from the conversation unless spoken to directly.

Bee attempted to draw him out first by teasing, then by openly flirting with every man that came near them. To save his own embarrassment at her behaviour, Roger began to thaw a little. Besides, he had caught sight of himself reflected in the darkened window. He looked unhappy, and he must not give the game away. Bee was ridiculous; Graham a fool; Catherine a nervous wreck. He suddenly found the whole scenario hilarious. Roger decided to get drunk, maybe he would pluck up the courage to tell them all how he felt. Maybe.

Unaware of Roger's inward hilarity, the rest of the company chatted on inanely, batting their silly slights and snobberies across the table. Catherine noticed a couple making their way purposefully towards them. Looking up she saw the welcome face of Floss with, she presumed, her dinner partner, a man of around forty, dressed in country tweeds.

"It's Floss," she turned to Bee. "Remember, at the Antique Fair?"

"Oh yes," smirked Bee. Turning to Roger and Graham, she continued, "Don't get too excited, she runs the Burger Bar!"

Graham sniggered. Floss and her companion were at their table and must have heard Bee's aside.

Catherine blushed. "How good to see you," she said, half standing.

"Don't get up," protested Floss, "I couldn't just walk past since we spotted you. I thought I should come over and say hello."

"Let me introduce my husband, Graham," Catherine said, "and our neighbours, Bee and Roger."

Floss nodded her acknowledgement.

"We've met," she smiled at Bee. Bee nodded grudgingly. Floss went on to introduce the man at her side. "And this tall, dark and handsome stranger is my brother-in-law, Andrew. We often eat out on Saturday evenings. Thought we would try somewhere a bit further afield today."

Andrew was indeed tall, dark and handsome, in a lanky, unconventional, curly-haired, blue-eyed way. He smiled at Catherine; his gaze lingered as if he were surprised at what he saw. Surprised and delighted.

"Spending the takings, eh?" laughed Bee, with ill-disguised contempt. "They don't do burgers and chips here, you know!"

Graham laughed. "Very sharp is our Bee," he said, putting his hand out to shake Andrew's hand. "Graham Chandler," he intoned solemnly, "Sales Director for Centaur Plastics."

He said it as if expecting a response, and when none was forthcoming, asked Andrew what he did for a living. Catherine was becoming more and more embarrassed by the moment. Lowly as Graham and the others considered these people to be, they deserved more respect than this. Andrew's reply that he 'dabbled in this and that, local heritage, land, antiques,' elicited an arch look, accompanied with few knowing taps to the side of the nose from Graham, and a sotto voce, "Gypsies," from the inebriated Bee to Roger.

Floss winced at this casual, offhand bigotry but before she could respond, Catherine jumped up from her seat, "Thank you so much for taking the trouble to come over."

"No trouble at all." Floss swallowed her words, and turned away to follow the waiter to their table. "Have a good evening, Catherine."

Andrew inclined his head in an old-fashioned bow. "Good evening, Catherine." He smiled at her alone, his eyes meeting hers. Catherine was taken aback; surely, he wasn't flirting with her. What a preposterous idea! She blushed at the thought as she sat down. The other three had not missed this little inter-play.

"Ooh! Cath's got an admirer," mocked Bee. "The Gypsy King!"

She almost choked on her gin as Graham responded, "And the Burger Queen!"

The conversation continued in this hilarious vein for far longer than necessary. Catherine was ashamed of them. She watched as Floss and her brother were shown to their table. Their eyes met again as Andrew looked up from his menu. Catherine turned quickly away and spent the remainder of the evening assiduously avoiding his gaze. She thought herself silly, as if he would even think it look in her direction again. Nevertheless, she felt very aware of his presence and was glad when they finally left the restaurant.

Three

By Monday morning, Catherine was glad to see Graham off to work. She began the day as usual on a Monday, with changing the sheets and doing the washing. To her, this weekly ritual of cleaning the house after the weekend was like reclaiming her territory after Graham's invasion. Wash the sheets, wash him away. Tidy him away along with his discarded clothes. He had never allowed her to work. She once had a 'little job' as he called it, when the children were both at school, but she began to form opinions and make friendships which were outside of his control. This was when he first started to berate her house-keeping abilities. He would point out her slovenliness. He called her selfish for pursuing her own interests at the expense of the home and family. She was soon persuaded to give up the job and become a full-time housewife. Not that she minded. Catherine was always busy, the house immaculate, the garden well-tended, the larder always full.

By mid-morning the house was spotless and the washing on the line. Catherine made herself a cup of tea and sat at the kitchen table to read yesterday's papers before packing them up for the recycle bin. She loved the Sunday supplements, from the impracticably white-carpeted homes in the 'Style' section to the far distant hotels in 'Travel.' Each Monday morning found her reading every section from cover to cover.

*****

John was on the phone to Simon. His grandson regularly phoned to let him know how things were going, and to ask for advice on the situations he often came up against. As a child Simon enjoyed long walks on the common with John and his dog, Deefer. These were precious times sharing stories, asking advice and 'putting the world to rights,' as John would say. As Simon grew older the walks continued, the grandfather and grandson growing ever closer through a shared faith, affection and mutual respect. Deefer was old and arthritic now, and walks on the common were a less frequent event for both him and his owner, but the conversations between John and Simon continued with the same light tone and deep understanding.

*****

Graham Chandler was at the office, at work selling himself. He was undeniably a gifted salesman. Even as a young man he could fawn and flatter and dance and delight, until the customer was hypnotised into a purchase. Now of course, he dealt only with the 'big boys.' Somehow, his particular blend of sycophantic snobbery appealed to his mirror images in so many big companies. He had risen into the company stratosphere by sheer lust for status. And now, in his early fifties, Graham was swimming with the big fish. A Sales Director, his management style meant he surrounded himself with his own reflections: ambitious, ruthless, and remorseless.

Now Graham had achieved the status, the salary, the company car, he wanted the image to be complete. He looked around him. He saw what other people had and wanted it. Yet there was something that eluded him, something he could not purchase or learn or seem to absorb. There was no name for it, an attitude, a way of being that Graham Chandler perpetually struggled for, yet consistently failed to attain. If pushed to put a label on it, Graham would call it 'class,' or 'breeding,' which perfectly demonstrated he had neither.

Graham knew that Catherine had this elusive quality for which he yearned so much. In fact, it was what drove him to her at first. He wanted to be what she so easily was, and when he realised he could not obtain her grace, he plotted to destroy it. He was in a perpetual state of jealousy. It seemed to him that despite his power over her, his betrayal and spite served only to illuminate both her character and his.

*****

Catherine bundled up the week's newspapers for recycling and took them out to the green box. As she went to open the lid, the phone rang. Catherine jumped with shock. She dropped the papers which scattered across the floor. As she picked up the phone, she recognised Graham's cough. The guilty cough which always preceded a lie. Why he should feel uncomfortable, since he was such a practised liar, she did not know. But she knew the words before he said them. Graham would be late, don't wait up, and so the script went on. She could remember her lines and repeat them as expected.

"Okay. No, that's not a problem. Drive safely." Then, curiously, she was filled with anger. She thought she heard a laugh as Graham said goodbye and reached to put the handset in its cradle.

"Graham!" she shouted, "Graham!"

He put the receiver back to his ear with a sigh, "What?"

"Sorry, did you say something"

"What?"

"I thought you said something else, after you said goodbye." She began to lose her nerve. What was she thinking?

"No. Don't be a fool, Catherine."

"I'm not a fool, Graham. I know exactly what's going on."

"What do you mean by that?" He sounded affronted.

Catherine was pleased. "I mean, I understand that you have to work late. Bye." She hung up and began to breathe again.

It surprised Catherine that she shook a little as she knelt to pick up the scattered papers. It surprised her more that she began to cry. She wondered why these things still hurt. "Silly girl," she muttered, and wiped her eyes.

That is when she saw the advertisement: Westbury's Antiques, Art and Collectibles, 24-28 New James Street, London W1 - *Auction of Antique Pottery, Curios, Staffordshire China and Toby Jugs.*

She smiled as she imagined herself at an auction. As she packed the newspapers away into their box, she packed the imagined adventure away too. Graham would never agree to it.

She smiled to herself; there was something about that jug. Graham scorned it, just as he did her. Maybe that was why she wanted to look after it. If she had to 'get rid of it' as Graham had so loudly insisted, then she would at least make sure it went to someone who would appreciate it. If there was an auction of Toby jugs, then there must be collectors of Toby jugs. Catherine went upstairs and released the jug from her hiding place in the dressing table. She really was very fine. Her plumed hat and faint smile gave her an air of virtuous self-satisfaction. This Toby jug had personality and style; she was much too good for a jumble sale. The telephone rang. Catherine reached across the bed to answer it. Bee's familiar squawk pierced her eardrum.

"It's me, I need to go to town; I'm desperate for some voile for the bathroom window. Besides, I'm bored silly here. My cleaner comes at eleven. I don't think I can face another boring conversation about her stupid family. I might get a manicure while I'm there, cheer myself up. Can you bring the car round here? Save me getting gravel in my strappy sandals. Ten minutes alright?"

Catherine looked at the face of the little jug in her hand. "I'm sorry Bee," she stated, firmly, "You'll have to take a taxi, I have other plans. I'll see you later, maybe."

She hastily replaced the handset before her new resolve deserted her. With unaccustomed determination, Catherine carefully wrapped the jug in several head scarves, ran downstairs, put it into her large handbag and headed for the car. Catherine hurried up the drive and jumped into the car, not stopping to put on her seat belt until she was half-way up the street. Bee was tottering with speed along the road behind her, cursing and shouting. Catherine hoped there were no stones in her strappy sandals.

*****

She pulled into the railway station and before her resolve melted away bought a ticket to London. It was only when she was on the train that the enormity of her actions dawned on her. She laughed to herself as she remembered Bee comically in pursuit of the car. The man in the seat opposite stood up suddenly and moved to another seat. Catherine caught sight of herself in the window as the train entered a tunnel. She was wearing an old sloppy jumper over a shapeless ethnic skirt. There were two clothes pegs attached to the front of her jumper and, to her horror, as she looked at her feet, she saw she was wearing her slippers! The ridiculousness of the situation grabbed her again and she began to laugh out loud. "I *am* the loony on the train!" She chuckled to herself.

After a short journey, Catherine squeezed herself between the purposeful shoppers and dithering tourists until she emerged into the London sunshine. She decided to head for the nearest department store and do something about her bag-lady appearance. As she riffled through the tidy rails, she suddenly had to stop. A long-forgotten feeling surged through her, not unfamiliar, but so far distant she had to reach back to the edge of her memory to recognise it. And suddenly, there it was, like a laughing friend...*freedom*! She inhaled the feeling and held on to it, and the power of that moment filled her up. How odd, to have a life changing moment amongst the knitwear. Now the germ of rebellion was planted. Now the disease would grow.

Catherine had no idea what to buy, she was so used to buying safe, plain and unremarkable, usually purchased after an exhausting day's shopping, trailing in Bee's wake. The sight of Bee's improbably young clothes on her reconstructed body was always enough to send Catherine scuttling for the 'classic style' antidote for herself. Hence Bee's wardrobe was stuffed with designer trash and Catherine's with plain and prudent separates. Catherine glared at the oatmeal shirt dress she was about to buy and thrust it back on the rail with disgust.

"I don't want safe and boring anymore," she muttered to herself "I don't want classic". Catherine picked up and immediately replaced a floral tunic with contrasting leggings, then a black twinset and pleated skirt, then a pair of grey slacks and long cardigan. "No! No! No! "She despaired. "I don't want black, or beige or grey, I don't want *old*, I don't want invisible…what *do* I want!?"

As she looked hopelessly about her, Catherine gazed at the mannequins in coordinated splendour. A bright dress with a full skirt and contrasting cardigan appealed to her newly emancipated self. It occurred to her that she could do worse than copy the look in its entirety. At least she would be dressed in some sort of style, if not exactly her own. So, half an hour later, a distinctly different Catherine, newly suited, booted, and shockingly curvaceous, stood smiling on the Oxford Street pavement. The clothes she had travelled in were in a carrier bag, which she held at her side. Without hesitation, Catherine squashed the lot into a bin outside the shop, hailed a taxi and travelled to Westbury's.

Arriving outside Westbury's Auction House, Catherine patted her handbag

"Well, Martha, it's now or never" she whispered as she stood at the foot of the well-trodden sandstone steps. "Courage! Don't fail me now." Then, taking a deep breath, she marched up the steps, pushed open the heavy glass door and walked into a cavernous, white-marbled entrance hall.

The sheer size and grandeur of the place took her breath away. She looked about her. Forty feet ahead stood a vast mahogany desk, jutting out from between the two staircases like the bow of some ice-bound ship. At the helm of this imposing structure stood a tall, thin, expressionless woman in a sombre suit. Around her flitted two or three younger clones of herself, identically dressed, equally devoid of character. One leafed through a catalogue, answering a query no doubt. Catherine caught her eye and smiled; the clone looked away. The place was busy; people approached the formidable ship's captain with no apparent fear. Others strode purposefully towards the various doorways leading from the corridors. Some even mounted the stairs. Everyone seemed to know exactly where to go, and to be completely un-awed by their splendid surroundings. As she watched, Catherine's confidence leaked away.

"I'm an idiot!" she told herself. "People bring gold cups and Old Masters here, not silly little pottery jugs. Graham will kill me." She could hear him now laughing at her naïveté, calling her a time waster. "Stupid, stupid woman," she told herself. "Stupid, stupid, me."

With nothing on her mind but the need to escape quickly, Catherine turned sharply and headed for the door, bumping straight into a man who had just walked in. He was carrying some sort of folder along with his briefcase. Or rather he had been carrying it until Catherine knocked it out of his hand. Papers spilled across the floor. "I'm so sorry, I'm so sorry," was all she could say, again and again, as she helped to retrieve them. Her face was red with embarrassment.

"Please don't apologise." he said. "I wasn't looking where I was going. It's my fault entirely." She looked up, replacing the last sheet of paper. It was Andrew, Floss' brother-in-law. "Hello!" he smiled "Its Catherine isn't it? My sister Florence introduced us at the restaurant." He looked at her new outfit with admiration. "You're looking very nice, today."

Catherine blushed even more at the memory of that evening. "Yes, Catherine Chandler," she stammered, tongue tied and self-conscious, lost for words. Then, realising he was speaking to her again, she had to pull in every ounce of concentration and self-control to listen. He had asked, of course, why she was here. Catherine, calmer than she had been, explained that she had brought something to be valued.

"It all seemed so simple in my kitchen," she said ruefully, "a bit of an adventure, but the reality is rather daunting. I had just decided to forget it, when I bumped into you. Literally!" They both laughed.

He touched her arm, "Come on, I'll show you the ropes." He guided her towards the mahogany galleon and called across to the 'Captain.'

"Miss Buckling, is George Phillips available, do you know?"

The lady leaned forward, she actually smiled. "He is, sir, in the Chinese room. I'll let him know you are coming." She glanced curiously at Catherine as she picked up the telephone receiver.

Andrew led Catherine down one of the panelled corridors. "Follow me" he said.

"You seem to be very well known here," Catherine said, a little breathlessly as she half ran at his side.

"I'm often in Town," he replied.

She had hoped for more information, but did not wish to pry, or to appear unnaturally interested. Which, of course, she was. Perhaps this was one of the 'this and that' he had mentioned. Maybe he was a collector himself. Before she could find out any more about him, they had arrived at the doorway to what she assumed was the Chinese Room. Andrew curved his arm behind her to open the door. He put his other arm on her shoulder as he greeted the Valuer who approached them.

"George," he called. "This lady has an item you might like to take a look at." Andrew smiled at her "Catherine, I'll leave you in George's capable hands." Before either she or George Phillips could speak a word, Andrew had politely made his goodbyes and left.

Andrew, leaning against the wall outside the valuation room, needed a few moments to regain his balance. Catherine had just, almost literally, knocked him off his feet, which was a fairly accurate representation of her impact on him since their first meeting.

He thought of her often and his interest had grown with every anecdote from Floss. He had told himself that he was just a sucker for a damsel in distress, that this was a silly mid-life crush and above all that Catherine was another man's wife, albeit a jumped-up scoundrel who did not deserve her. Today, though, in all her glorious curves and unconscious, blushing beauty, she had captivated him all over again.

A passing worker, seeing him apparently frozen in place, asked if he could be of any assistance. With a deep breath and a shake of the head, Andrew thanked the young man for his concern and set off with purpose to nowhere in particular. "Pull yourself together, man!" he chided himself.

From his side of the desk inside the Chinese Room George Phillips looked at Catherine expectantly. She realised he was waiting to see the object in question. "Thank you so much for seeing me," she said, fumbling in her bag and finally removing the large bundle of scarves from within. Mr Phillips was completely unmoved, as if flustered fat ladies disgorged the contents of their handbags for him every day. She unwrapped the Toby jug and handed it over.

"I found her at an antique fair," she explained. "She's probably not worth much, but I liked her so much I couldn't resist."

She paused for breath. The expert turned the jug this way and that. Cupping it in his hands, he turned it over and inspected the base. Closing his eyes, he ran his fingers over the surface, examining the whole jug intimately, paying particular attention to the rim, the handle, the base. It made a pleasant change for him to see someone who had bought for pleasure rather than gain.

"You are not in the antiques business, I take it," said George, softly.

"Goodness me, no." Catherine looked surprised. "A friend dragged me to the market. I spotted this while I was there. Much as I love it, my husband insists she's only fit for the rubbish tip. I wanted her to go to a good home." She laughed, weakly, "Silly, isn't it!"

George Phillips gave a mischievous smile. "Not at all, not at all silly. What would you like to know about her?"

Catherine returned his smile, relaxed and enthused. "Anything. I know nothing about Toby jugs. I just like her. Is a lady Toby unusual? I've never heard of one. Why does she look so happy? How old is she? What's her story?" Catherine stopped for breath. "Sorry," she said, "I'm getting carried away with myself!"

George Phillips looked up from his exploration of the treasure he held in his hands. "As far as I can tell," he said, softly, "this is a near perfect, mid-eighteenth century, Toby Jug, representing one Martha Gunn. Martha helped rich ladies to bathe in those funny things that looked like beach huts on wheels."

"A type of servant, then?" Catherine asked.

"More than that," said George Phillips. "She was held in high regard. Bathing was medicinal rather than recreational in those days. Martha was a nurse of sorts, I suppose." He held up Martha Gunn. "There aren't many of these about, you know. Do you have it insured?"

Catherine's face fell. "Much as I'd like to, I can't keep her," she confided. "My husband hates her. He wanted me to throw poor Martha in the dustbin."

"You have a very good eye, Mrs Chandler, excellent taste. Your husband might change his mind if he knew how much this piece could be worth. This one is a little smaller than I expected. It may once have been part of a set."

Catherine clapped her hands together with joy. "I knew there was something special about her!" Catherine's excitement and anticipation became almost uncontainable. She stood up, hugging those words of praise to herself: a good eye, excellent taste. She thought, I did something right! She was surprised at her own surprise.

Mr Phillips raised his eyebrows, looking over his spectacles at her, and quietly asked, "Would you like a valuation?"

Catherine walked across to the window, remembered Graham's fury at her 'waste of good money.' She could make amends by paying him back.

"Yes, I would like a valuation, please Mr Phillips."

George Phillips looked over his spectacles at her. "What sort of price were you hoping for?"

"As I paid £50, I'll be happy to make that, and to know she'll be in safe hands."

"I think we can guarantee that," Mr Phillips chuckled. "A lot of collectors would give their eye teeth for a piece as good as this. We'll put a reserve on it of £750. It could well go for twice that. I take it you're not familiar with our procedures?"

Catherine shook her head, dumbstruck.

"I'll call someone to help you." He hailed some helpful assistant, and before Catherine knew it, she was outside the big yellow building once again, having left Martha Gunn, with corresponding forms, in the safe keeping of one of Mr Phillips' careful experts

*****

Catherine stood, shaken, on the steps of the auction house. She walked down the steps in a daze and headed for home. As she headed for Oxford Street and the tube, she thought she heard her name called. As she turned, there was Floss! After their mutually surprised and delighted greetings, Floss asked if the dreaded Bee was likely to pop up at any moment. Catherine was pleased tell Floss that she had abandoned Bee, fuming, in her driveway.

The look on Floss' face was one of shocked amusement. "You mean you just left her there, in a cloud of dust and exhaust fumes?"

Catherine felt suddenly ashamed. "I suppose it was a bit unkind," she said, biting her lip, "but..."

"I think it's hilarious!" interrupted Floss, "and absolutely just!" She thrust her arm through Catherine's. "Come on I know a decent pub just a short walk from here. Let's get lunch and you can tell me all the gory details!"

As they enjoyed their meal, Floss listened with amusement to the story of Catherine's stunning sartorial transformation. "So, the whole lot is in a bin outside

Debenhams," Catherine giggled, "and you see before you a new woman, in polka dots!"

"Yes, who would guess what was hiding under those baggy jumpers and sensible skirts?" she said with raised eyebrows.

Catherine, worried, asked, "What do you mean, hiding?"

"I mean that tiny waist," Floss grinned, pointing to her cinched-in midriff, then raising her finger a few inches, "and those!" she grinned. Catherine, trying not to look pleased at the compliment, went to button her cardigan. Leaning forward conspiratorially, Catherine whispered

"I'm wearing a," she blushed "a foundation garment, the lady in the shop recommended it. 'Shapewear' they call it"

Floss nodded, the mystery explained "Harvest Festivals" she said, "that's what I call them"

"Harvest Festivals?" Catherine asked, puzzled'

"All is safely gathered in!" Floss answered with a mischievous smile.

Catherine laughed, but looking down at her newly acquired curves, began to have second thoughts.

"Is it too much?" she asked Floss. She imagined Graham's mockery "Do I look ridiculous?"

"Not at all," Floss smiled, "you look perfectly elegant and proper, but there's no disguising it, you are a bombshell!"

"Bombshell?" Catherine asked, "You mean like the old movie stars, Mae West, Marylin Monroe, you don't see many of them about these days"

"You obviously don't watch enough daytime TV", said Floss in mock disapproval, going on to list a host of actors, presenters, pop stars and a celebrity chef notorious for her indulgent recipes and luscious beauty.

"Bombshells every one of them," she said, "as are you"

"Oh, my word," Catherine said, striking a pose.

"From bag-lady to bombshell in one morning, it sounds like a self-help book"

"Maybe you should write one" Floss said "You have a gift for telling a tale". She looked at her watch, "I'm so sorry, but I will have to go soon, I'm meeting Andrew at two."

To Floss's consternation, Catherine groaned and dropped her head into her hands, saying "Oh, I didn't get to *that* part of the story yet." She looked up, wincing, "I bumped into Andrew this morning," she said "and I mean I did, actually, bump into him. Poor man" As she paid the bill and they left the pub, Catherine quickly described the encounter at Westbury's.

"I'm sure Andrew was very happy to see you again," Floss assured her, as they hugged goodbye outside the pub, "and I'll look forward to hearing his version of the event," she said, with a wry smile.

Catherine had chosen not to tell Floss about Martha Gunn. She had said, simply, that she had taken a vase to be valued. Catherine wanted to hug that secret to herself for a little longer. Besides, Floss would never understand that Catherine was giving up the Toby Jug purely because Graham would not allow her to keep it.

She thought of Graham. Of course, she could not tell him. It would be gloating. It would hurt his feelings, his pride. Then he would twist it all round so she was wrong and he was right. There always had to be a wrong and a right for Graham, someone to blame. No, she decided, this is my secret, my secret triumph. I won't let him spoil it and I'll just give him his £50 back!

*****

As Catherine was beginning the long road back to her true self, her husband was taking the rather shorter route to his usual self. Graham Chandler shook the hand of his most recently acquired customer. Weeks of gentle nurture, building, tempting, ingratiating had finally been rewarded. Another respectably large account added to his credit; another star on his board, back at Head Office. As he climbed into his vintage sports car, he thought of their reaction to his latest sale. He was still the unbeaten king of the sales department, with top sales for the past five years in a row. Serious clients, serious money. He sped along the motorway, savouring his triumph, as he

61

barked the office number and was immediately connected.

"This is Graham Chandler, give me extension 245." The receptionist put him through. "Come on, come on, pick up, for God's sake" he muttered.

"I'm afraid that line is busy at this time, can you hold?"

"No, I can't hold, time is money. Give me extension 246." This time the call was answered. "Graham Chandler. Who am I talking to...? Well, young Jenny, I want to speak to Miss Belton as soon as she is available. Could you please ask her to call me back, soonest?" He hung up, cutting off young Jenny's flow of apology and promise.

He had to tell someone about his latest conquest. He began to recite his home number, then cancelled and switched on the radio instead. Graham turned the radio up louder. He did not want to think about anything. The meaning of life, and all that, meaning nothing. "YES!" he yelled, laughing, "I am the greatest!" He sang loudly along with the radio.

A service station loomed ahead. Graham took the slip road and found a parking space. As he walked up the steps, he saw himself reflected in the big glass windows. He liked what he saw. A successful man, looking less than his years, he had often been told. Expensively dressed, immaculately coiffed, manicured and tanned - the picture of success. He smiled to himself.

"I've still got it," he thought.

The doors opened out onto a marketplace in miniature. A slot machine arcade was filled with sullen, but evidently well-financed adolescents. A virtual ski-slope bearing a scruffy 'out of order' notice written in green biro, was off to one side. Graham could choose from American style fast food (with English style slow service), sticky buns and open sandwiches from the 'eatery', or waitress service at the 'Cut Above Carvery' which, naturally, was on the top floor. Graham elected for the latter. Pushchairs and coach parties tend to avoid stairs. First, though, he had a promise to keep.

He weaved his way through the scattered groups of people, stopping outside a window filled with richly coloured scarves, wraps and ties. A smile played on his fleshy lips as he padded inside and stroked his fingers through the merchandise. So much choice. A too cheery, over made-up shop assistant approached him.

"Have you seen anything you'd like, sir?" she smiled.

Graham's smile became a salacious grin, as he looked her over. "Most definitely," he almost licked his lips, "but I think I'll just buy a scarf."

The mature assistant giggled girlishly, inwardly squirming, "How can I help you, sir?"

"I need something special, a gift for a lady. Something stylish" He plucked a diaphanous oblong from its holder. "I like this, but maybe something bigger."

"A wrap maybe. Ladies love them, sir. Very versatile, very stylish."

"Show me," said Graham, peremptorily. She reached up to a series of golden hoops just above her head, and pulled out three or four swathes of semi-transparent, shimmering colour. Peacock colours, spice colours, jewel colours, all fell from her hands like water.

"Nice." he said. "I'll take the blue one."

As he returned to the car, well fed from the 'Cut Above Carvery,' his phone rang. He lifted it to his ear, glancing around to see how many people had noticed that he was using one of the latest designs in mobile phones.

"Hello, gorgeous, what took you so long? ... Yeah, clinched it!" He preened with satisfaction as Miss Mandy Belton relayed the news to the rest of the office, who dutifully cheered and clapped. A chorus of 'nice one!' and a triumphal 'YES!' squeaked through the earpiece.

"Obviously you're not alone, sweetie,"

"That's absolutely correct, Mr Chandler."

"Very efficient, darling. Can we meet later, a little celebration?"

"I really don't think that's very likely, Mr Chandler, do you?"

"Mandy, it's just dinner. Somewhere special. Go on, you'll love it."

"Well…"

"I promise, just a meal together. I'm on a high. I can't just go home. You know what it's like there."

"Rather dull, I believe," she laughed.

He laughed too. "Exactly! Go on, Mandy, I'll be good. I promise."

"In that case, I'm sure I can arrange that, Mr Chandler. What time would that be, do you think?"

"I'll be at the Haywain Hotel in about an hour. Can you meet me there?"

"Yes, that should be fine. I'll be leaving at five today, Mr Chandler, so I will see you in the morning. Congratulations on your success!"

Graham was buzzing. His skin tingled with the thrill, the intrigue. As he drove to the hotel, he congratulated himself on his power to attract. One more phone call to make. He shouted his home number and swore as the answering machine kicked in. On the other hand, it was even easier to lie to a machine. He left the usual message. Graham was a top-class salesman, varnishing the truth, or obliterating it altogether, came so easily to him. A skill finely honed and perfected over years, to charm a client, to bewitch a lover, to deceive a wife. No problem.

*****

Standing impatiently behind her fashionable voile drapes, looking through the window, Bee waited for Catherine to return. As the car pulled up, she threw open the door and flounced out. Catherine had a satisfied look to her as she locked the car and turned to walk up the drive. She jumped at Bee's shrill, "At last, the wanderer returns!" Bee stomped down the drive towards her. Catherine stepped away from the car with a sigh and began to walk indoors.

"Catherine! Catherine!" shrilled Bee, pursuing Catherine up the path, her high heels unsteady, clacking and clattering on the slate paving.

"Catherine!" Clack! Clack! "Catherine!" Clacketty-clacketty, click, click. "I had to get a taxi you know. You can be so selfish. You didn't tell me…" Pock, pock, pock, her little pointy shoes pierced the gravel and clattered onto the steps. She was almost face-to-face with Catherine, emitting a choking mist of some designer scent. Catherine coughed. She opened the door and was immediately followed in by Bee.

"Do come in," Catherine said, putting her bag on the table. Bee was rather non-plussed by Catherine's demeanour. No stumbling apology, no polite excuse. Truthfully, Catherine was just too tired to speak, but the effect on Bee was surprising. Catherine filled the kettle.

"Tea?" she asked brightly, aware that Bee was simmering with suppressed anger. She wondered how it would surface. Sometimes Bee snapped off sharp little shards of spite, hurling them from behind little conversational pleasantries until her rage was all used up. Sometimes she piled up all her imagined hurts into a slow burning bonfire of reproach, leaving Catherine hot with unnecessary self-reproach. This time there could be no justification for a direct attack. "After all, "Catherine thought, "I am not at her beck and call. I can do what I want." Of course, she would never dare say this to Bee. Bee would be hurt, and Catherine would rather not cause a scene.

Bee had evidently decided to ooze. She hissed and bubbled with spite, simpering, strangely flirtatious. If Catherine had not been so concerned with Bee's opinion of her, if she had not been so ready to take the blame for Bee's imagined pain, she would have dismissed her. Instead, Catherine found herself mesmerised.

"Well, we have been a long time at our 'other arrangements' young Catherine, haven't we?"

Catherine laughed nervously and handed her interrogator a cup of tea.

"Go on then Cath, where did you go? You've been hours. Never gave poor old Bee a second thought! Off gallivanting!"

"I just fancied some time by myself. You know…a day out." She misjudged the height of the table. The mug of tea spilled as it banged down too hard.

"No need to be so jumpy, Cath. I know just what you mean. All the same, you could have asked me along. I was desperate to go to the shops. I had to get a taxi in the end, and then I was so flustered I hardly bought a thing! I don't know why you thought I'd be in the way. Anyway, it must have been something very important to make you leave your only friend in the lurch!"

"Not really. I just wanted to be on my own today. It was an impulse thing,"

Bee mimicked a German accent, "I vant to be alone!" Contempt and smiles raced to her lips simultaneously. The smile just slipped in first as her eyes swept Catherine from her shoes to her face. "We are mysterious, dear and what's with the new look?"

Bee had become aware of the change in Catherine's appearance; it made her feel uncomfortable. "Have you had some sort of style transplant?"

Catherine giggled. She had to break her gaze. She turned away and reached for the biscuit tin. "Garibaldi?" She twisted off the lid and offered the contents to Bee.

Bee stroked her hands over her hips, "Ooh no, not for me, but you don't need to bother. Go ahead."

Catherine gave the half full barrel a little shake, expertly flipping the contents, revealing the hidden layer. Nothing appealed to her. She replaced the lid and slid the tin to the end of the table. Bee continued her whining, probing, sulking.

"I don't know why you're being so secretive..." Suddenly her eyes widened, she gaped as if shocked. "Surely not!" Her eyes narrowed, locking on to Catherine's, then she blasted out a great guffaw of a laugh. "For a moment there, I almost suspected you of having a secret lover. Hoo, hoo, hoo!" she laughed, apparently unable to contain herself. "Don't make me laugh!"

Catherine looked, and was, hurt. Was it really so very preposterous an idea? Bee's eyes were streaming. "Don't get in a huff, you daft bat! Hoo, hoo, hoo! It's not very likely is it? Be honest!"

"I suppose not," Catherine mumbled.

Bee rose to go. Catherine smiled, relieved; at least the questions had finished.

"Can't wait to tell Graham," Bee smirked, still chuckling, grotesquely. "He'll die laughing!"

Catherine showed Bee out, both smiling. She leaned against the door exhausted.

Lately it seemed that each day fell monotonously into yesterday. Her mind cast across the rest of the day. Today had been a good day, an adventure, a day she had not wanted to end. Catherine could not remember the last time she did not want a day to be over.

Four

Catherine knew the moment she noticed the answer phone winking at her, snatching her away form the happy memories. Of course she did. It was like the helter-skelter at the funfair. There you go, sliding full tilt down to the inevitable bump at the end, only to pick up your mat and run like an idiot up the stairs for another fall. He was so glib, so cheerful. Graham was always cheerful when he lied. You could hear him smiling.

"Sorry darling, going to be unavoidably late, I'm afraid. Got to keep the pennies rolling in, work, work, work! Don't wait up. See you later... Oh, could you get my blue-striped shirt ready. I think it's in the wash. Big meeting tomorrow. Power dressing, and all that. See you!"

She pressed the delete button. Even Graham's betrayal was a sad repetition, and Catherine was surprised that this time it hardly hurt at all. It made her feel something, yes, but Catherine could not pin the feeling down. As if giving it a label would sort things out, tidy them up and wipe them away.

As Catherine put away the ironing board and hung up the freshly ironed shirt, her husband was only twenty miles away helping Mandy Belton to choose her main course. This lady needed no help, unlike the silly young things Graham usually wined, dined and bedded. Mandy knew exactly what she wanted; from the menu, from her job, from her life. Graham, simpering, fawning Graham would have been startled to find out his own part in Miss Belton's ambitions.

She was small and short; those who flattered her called her petite. Her rich, chestnut brown hair had been skilfully coloured and styled away from its natural pale brown mop. She dressed with style, mock cashmere and silk, rather than the brash acid-coloured polyesters chosen by Grahams usual 'girls,' with her make up understated, her manner at once cool and inviting.

Mandy did not hand the menu to Graham in awe, asking him to order. Instead, she beckoned the hovering waiter, ordered decisively and looked wryly across at her flustering partner. Graham chose his meal to impress Mandy, who had chosen what she wanted, and who was apparently unaware and equally unimpressed by his choice. He handed her the gift he had so carefully chosen, store-wrapped in gold coloured paper, embossed with the designer logo.

"I have been thinking about you," he whispered, warmly. Mandy thanked him quietly and put the package, unopened, into her handbag. "Aren't you going to open it?" he begged. "It's just a little token of my esteem."

She looked around, as if to make sure no one was watching. Then retrieving the gift, she quickly prised open one corner, pulled out a little of the fabric inside. "It's very nice," she said, with an attempt at a smile. "Thank you."

Graham could not fail to be hurt and distinctly amazed at this unexpected response. It had always worked. They were always impressed. Why not Mandy?

"It's a scarf thing. A wrap I think they called it. I thought you'd like it."

"I do. Thank you," she answered him, painfully polite. She smiled inwardly, watching him squirm on the hook.

He could not stand it anymore. His outburst sounded like a sulky teenaged lover, "You don't! It's obvious you don't. What's wrong with it? Other women would love a…"

She raised a forbidding hand. "That's right Graham. Other women, and lots of them, no doubt. You need to know that I am not some quick tumble from the office. If that's not okay, then a good working relationship is all we have."

He was struck dumb. No one dared to talk to him this way. Not even his wife. Least of all his wife. He felt angry, humiliated, intrigued. He had to have her, whatever it took. He would promise her anything, he didn't have to mean a word of it. Mandy had seen his discomfort, she revelled in it. She could see him turning her ultimatum over in his head. As she watched, he relaxed and leaned forward in his seat.

He looked into her eyes. "*Of course* it's okay, very okay, Mandy." He gave her a lascivious leer which he had intended to be a seductive smoulder. She took it as it was meant.

"Please tell me why you don't like the scarf, Mandy. It's got 'designer label' printed all over it. That scarf's not any old rubbish you know!" His tone was condescending; her swift answer, crushing.

"To be quite truthful, Graham, that's exactly the problem. Rather ostentatious for me, I'm afraid. Quality recognises quality; there is no need to advertise."

Their first course arrived, conveniently bringing the conversation to a close. He forced down snails in garlic butter, she savoured Coquilles St Jacques. After a while she spoke, building a bridge between them. Naturally, she expected him to walk across it to her. She did not intend to move.

"This is delicious, Graham," she breathed. "I didn't know this place existed. You've kept it all to yourself."

He felt forgiven, restored. He ran towards her, full tilt.

"I bring my special clients here," he replied, puffing himself up with pride. "It's not your run of the mill place you know. It's a classy place. Bloody expensive, but worth it. It's so important to make the right impression, Mandy. Can make the difference between getting a result or losing the game."

Mandy laughed softly, raising her eyebrows. "And what are you hoping for tonight, Graham?"

He deflated visibly. She laughed inside.

"Oh! I didn't mean…Well, not in that...I mean I'd like very, um…I, er… what I meant…"

She cut him short with a gesture. "I know what you mean, Graham. It is very nice that you want to impress me. I shall take it as a compliment."

She patted his hand, he grabbed hers, knocking over his white wine. The waiter hurried across to clean up the mess, replacing the shattered glass and blotting the table dry.

"Thank you," Mandy smiled graciously at the waiter as he left the table. She turned her eyes to meet Graham's.

"Are you alright?"

He sighed heavily, looking away. "This just isn't going as I expected." He was almost petulant.

Her tone was soothing. "Relax, darling, everything's fine. There's nothing to worry about. Relax and enjoy your meal." She reached across the table, giving his face the lightest stroke, then returned to her meal as if nothing had passed between them.

Graham was ecstatic, she was interested in him, she must be. She did not flirt, she had hardly touched him, yet he was filled with desire. He hung on her every word and gesture. She was well aware of the effect her presence had on him. She could go to a hotel room now and fulfil his wishes. They could have an affair which would burn out in a blaze of passion. It would be over in a few weeks or maybe months, but that was not enough this time.

Mandy liked to be in control. She had chosen Graham. He thought it was the other way around. She had plans for Graham. To catch him through his vanity would be so easy. Graham would reel himself in, given the right bait. The real skill would be to net him at last, unaware, gasping and thrashing onto the matrimonial bank. The fact that he was married was not an obstacle. Graham's philandering was legendary, his wife was a fool and he was ripe for catching. Mandy Belton was practised in her art and she meant to have Graham Chandler, all of him.

He drove home, enchanted, dizzy, infatuated. She had not even allowed him a farewell kiss. She had stood with her car door open as a barrier between them.

"Well done, Graham." She spoke as if he were an apprentice who had passed some qualifying test. "I had a pleasant evening. Let's do it again some time."

"Some time soon, I hope!" Graham had squeaked eagerly. He leaned over to kiss her cheek, but she dodged into her car and began to pull away.

"We'll see!" she called, as the window closed automatically.

In his own car Graham smiled inwardly, hugging himself. He had passed the test. It was very late when he finally slipped into bed beside Catherine.

*****

She feigned sleep, pushing anger and disappointment away. He was home, at least. She felt him look into her face and she held her breath. If she was asleep, there could be no argument, no lies to listen to, and no pain to feel. He dismissed her with a soft blasphemy, fell back onto his pillow and into deep satisfied sleep. Catherine lay awake, not dealing with her feelings. This had happened so many times before. Somehow, over the years, she had formed a strategy for dealing with the colossal wave of rejection that hit each time Graham betrayed her. Not just the other women, but with the constant, biting jibes which made up his speech to her. It was simple; she believed him. He said she was fat, clumsy inarticulate and she became so. He called her insecure, foolish, dull and she was. He turned to a mistress because Catherine had nothing to offer.

Coping with the sharpening of these feelings had become as familiar as unpacking the weekly shop. Same stuff, same packages.

First thing, top shelf: "I rise above it; after all he always comes home to me."

Next out of the bag was usually, "It's in his nature." Along with, "It's only a fling," and, "It doesn't mean anything to him."

Then, at Graham's suggestion, "I can't give him all he needs."

And down there at the bottom: "He needs me," squashed in beside "We're still together," and, but not quite so much lately, "I love him."

She packed and repacked her mantras, until she felt she had coped.

He woke with the alarm, swore and slid from the bed. Catherine lay apparently asleep as he hurried through his morning routine, eager to see Mandy. She heard him snatch the shirt from the hanger, with no attempt to let her sleep on. She made waking up movements, opened her eyes, but he was already on his way downstairs. She heard him grab his car keys and he was gone, the empty coat hanger still swaying. Catherine sat up in bed, put her hands over her eyes and sighed.

Graham pulled his company car with a flourish, if that were possible, into his designated parking space. It was early; he could see Mandy in the lobby chatting to the receptionist. He swaggered through the doors.

"I have some figures I need to discuss with you, when you're ready," he barked.

She turned on him in surprise. "I start at 8:45, Mr Chandler," she responded, apparently unmoved by his air of authority. "When I do, I'll let you know when I'm available."

The lift arrived, and he entered, turning to face her with an astonished glare. She had already resumed her conversation, and seemed oblivious to his presence, let alone his attitude. At around 9:15 a staff meeting was called, the usual 'get out there and win!' talk from the Managing Director. Finally, Graham was singled out for his most recent victory. Everyone clapped. He looked at Mandy; she smiled a half smile and turned away. He had expected the same adulation which gushed from the rest of the team. All the women made eyes at him. The men slapped his back; he was the star player. She stood up and gathered her papers.

"Here she comes," he congratulated himself. "She can't resist now."

Mandy walked towards him. "Nice work," she said. "Must get on now." With that she left. Leaving him marooned amongst a sea of handshakes and smiles. He ached to see her alone. Talk to her. Touch her. She fascinated him.

"I'm infatuated," he told himself, "and I love it." Graham anticipated the coming weeks with relish. Indeed, he licked his lips. This budding and blossoming of the affair he had always found the most exciting. Watching each of his women fall for him, he almost imagined himself in love too. As the blossoms fell and ripened into the heavy fruit of passion, as they became more committed, he would find his feelings withering away. Two or three weeks of, "My wife would kill herself if I left," usually meant they got the message. If not, a few professional words in the right ears would see the lovesick maiden transferred to another department. Graham's greatest love was himself. And love is blind.

Mandy stood at the window of the office and watched Graham drive away in his status symbol automobile. She felt not a shred of shame at having snared a married man. In fact, she rather congratulated herself on the fact that Graham thought their first liaison was all down to his charm, good looks and high position. Mandy was a realist, not a romantic. She had discovered as a very young girl how to charm anything she wanted from anyone who could give it to her.

No, Little Mandy had not been the school bully, or the school beauty, or the head girl, but she was even more powerful than any of them. And nobody knew it but her. Mandy had set her heart on being the second Mrs Graham Chandler, with all the status and wealth Graham boasted.

Five

Each day for Simon was a new day, a challenge and an adventure. His faith was stretched, his character enlarged, his calling confirmed; he was everything his father was not: sincere, dedicated, and open-hearted. He had his faults, naturally, but it was generally agreed by those who used the community centre that Simon Chandler was surprisingly normal for a religious man.

It was cold, this morning. Simon still missed the warmer southern mornings. It rained less there too, of course. That was, in Simon's view, about the most he could say for his childhood home. He had no homesick yearnings; he despised his father and pitied his pathetic mother. A soft, misty drizzle fell, wetting his face as he walked around to the front of the building. Rain had been the lifeblood of this city of cotton mills and coal mines. Now both industries had become distant history. Somewhere there was a 'genuine working mine' with guided tours and school visits. Tourists would take in 'the northern experience,' consisting of a canal ride to a former mill turned into a Millworks Museum and local Crafts Emporium, followed by the Coal Mine trip, finished off with a tour of Granada TV studios.

The other mines had long been filled in and grassed over; the few undemolished mills becoming Yuppie apartments, themed pubs or derelict shells. But the people remained. All those strapping 1960s lads and lasses, who, the Reformers said, would build a new future. Armed with their comprehensive school education, they had lived in the brand-new council estates, and had worked in the shops and offices which had competed fiercely in the thriving town centre. Sadly, forsaken by its own youth for three generations now, the town, 'urban renewed,' stuffed with Southern incomers, had no place for its native labourers.

Those who could go, did. Those who stayed mostly moved up the social scale and out of town, into the village style housing developments. Of those who remained, a good proportion, starved of their tradition, unsure of their place, drifted aimlessly into isolated hopelessness.

Simon looked across at his boss, 'Reverend Tim,' as everyone called him, who, with his devoted wife beside him, had dedicated his life to them. "There's no place for good honest hole diggers or box packers anymore," he sighed. "Everybody wants to be Mr Big."

"There's a place for them here, though," smiled Reverend Tim, "and they'll be here soon!" The two men parted company as the Minister left to visit the old folks' home and Simon went to open up the centre and prepare each room. Today would be busy with several activities and meetings running through the day and evening.

He unlocked the heavy steel shutters which protected the doors to the new extension. Today was his day in the Coffee shop. The place had been busy since it opened just before Christmas last year - friends dropping in; visitors; volunteers to serve and wash up, or just to chat; local people who dropped by for the company. He switched on the kettle to make himself a drink. His work at the project was more than work, it was a calling. He unlocked the cash register and counted out the float. Soon everything was set up and ready for the first visitors. Old Bill Campbell would be along soon. Bill usually dropped in for a coffee. Simon would often 'find' some new sandwich filling or cake sample which needed trying.

Bill a former soldier, had left the Army after his full twenty-two years' service to find Civvy Street had no place for him. He couldn't settle, did not belong. Living everywhere and nowhere, he worked from season to season in places where staff accommodation was provided and his rigid privacy could remain intact. He would disappear for months at a time, always returning eventually to St Christopher's, and the people he considered as family. Bill was always gracious, always kind and always immaculately scrubbed and polished, despite his vagrant lifestyle. Simon felt it a privilege to count this good gentleman as a friend. Bill was first to arrive at St Christopher's today, soaked; he must have been outside all night.

He came in and headed straight for the utility room. "Alright if I use the facilities, Vicar?" he called.

Simon was not a minister of the Church, ordained or otherwise, but Bill's use of the title held a significance understood by only the two of them.

Simon thought back to Christmas Eve two years ago, a night that changed them both for ever. It had been a really cold winter. Snow was predicted and many hoped for a white Christmas. That particular Christmas Eve, however, was disappointingly stormy, and the icy rain held no promise of snow. Staff, residents, and volunteers were all somewhere safe and warm. Simon, was in the Hall, finishing up the preparations for the Community Christmas Day Meal. It crossed his mind that Bill, who normally made a point of being there at Christmas, had not so far appeared.

He smiled as he thought of Bill, working away in the kitchen as others ate, and finally sitting down to a 'slap up feast' as he called it, once all the washing up was done and everyone else was drinking their final coffee. He would miss Bill this Christmas.

Simon turned to leave, turning off the lanterns on the Christmas tree then walking to the main entrance, he reached up to turn off the lights as he opened the heavy front door. As he did so, a dark figure fell into him, almost knocking him to the floor. Instinctively, Simon pushed the man back to see his face and recognised him immediately. "Bill!" He half carried the bedraggled, shivering and sobbing fellow indoors. Simon walked him to the bathroom, turned on the shower, and held Bill fully clothed under the hot spray. Gradually, the shivering and the sobbing subsided. Like a father caring for a frightened child, Simon tended to his friend. "Bill, you're safe now, you are home," he soothed, and finally, in fresh warm clothes, wrapped in a blanket, and holding a mug of sugary hot tea, the old soldier described his ordeal.

November 26th was his mother's birthday, and each year Bill would return to his home town, about fifty miles away, to 'pay his respects,' as he put it. The church there was evidently under new management, it would seem, as on this particular day, the church was open to visitors. Bill thought he would take a look inside the Church of his childhood. Simon looked into the eyes of this rigidly private, independent and broken man to see the remnants of the little boy within, speaking lovingly of his mother smiling at the few good memories of his past.

"Anyway," he said, "I went in, they were all very welcoming and invited me to come in for Sunday Service. So I did; and the next week, they were all over me, the Vicar even welcomed me on Sunday morning and Deidre, his wife, invited me for lunch." During that fateful lunch, under the guise of kindly interest, Deirdre and her husband interrogated Bill about his life, his work and the state of his soul. "It was like they wanted to fix me, like a project, a tick in their box." Bill wept. He had explained to them that he would stow his backpack and sleeping bag in a recess behind the pew at the open entrance to the church and go back there at night to sleep in the shelter of the big roof. "I wasn't a man anymore. I was 'the homeless.' I am not homeless; I live here and there, depending on where I'm working at the time. I don't bother anyone do I?"

Simon shook his head, sadly, "No Bill, you do not."

It was during a midweek visit to the church that Bill felt something was different. People looked at him, some hostile and some with pity. Hardly anyone spoke. Then, as Bill sat quietly with his tea, the lady behind the counter shouted across to Bill that Deirdre wanted a word with him in the office. She said 'The Office' as if it were the headmaster's study, or the gates of Hell.

It seemed to Bill that it was time to go, so instead of accepting her invitation, he headed for the door. All eyes were on him as he left. At the porch, he reached for his pack, safely hidden behind the pew. It was not there. He knelt to look under the pew in case it had fallen down, and as he did so he saw Deirdre standing in the doorway with a condescending smile on her face.

"We need to talk" she declared.

The humiliation of walking to the office through all the knowing faces at the coffee morning, became helpless rage as Deidre revealed that God had a plan for Bill's life which He had imparted to her during her 'quiet time' that morning. It seemed that the Good Lord had decided that all this lost sheep needed was a shove in the right direction, "to be housed, employed, and have a meaningful life," were Deirdre's exact words. She had arranged for him to be interviewed at the local charity for the homeless, and had bagged a place for him at the night shelter.

Bill informed her that if he needed her help he would have asked for it, that he would rather sleep under a hedge than in one of those filthy places filled with drugs and alcohol, and finally, "If you will kindly return my property, I will be on my way."

Deirdre was baffled. She knew what was best for 'these people,' and usually they complied, particularly if she started with "I believe the Lord would have me say…." After all, who would dare to argue with the Almighty? Indeed, Deirdre in compassionate mode was a force to be reckoned with. However, she hadn't reckoned with Bill, who calmly repeated his wish to get his things and go.

"I'm afraid that's not possible, Bill. I have thrown out those old things. It's time for a fresh start for you. I have prayed about this, and come on now, it's time we were at the shelter!"

And so it was that Bill had walked for two days in freezing rain. His scruffy, soaked, appearance meant it was impossible to hitch after the first day, or to spend more than a few minutes in any café or service station. Deirdre had disposed of his clothes and shaving kit along with his sleeping bag. He headed for St Christopher's, where he was just Bill, not a project.

Both men stayed at the hall that night as Bill told Simon more about himself, and how all he wanted to do was get on, with no interference, and causing as little trouble to other people as possible. "I would have been back here a week ago without those bloody Christians meddling in my life!" he complained.

Simon winced and Bill apologised for swearing. "Oh, it's not that," Simon sighed. "I think that lady's heart was in the right place, but…."

"Oh, she wasn't a real one," interrupted Bill, "and I know a real Christian when I see one, Simon."

"You do?" Simon asked.

"Yes, I see one every day at St Christopher's." Bill laughed at Simon's bemused expression.

"I'm looking at him!" roared Bill!

Since that night, Bill spent a lot more time at St Christopher's, often staying with Simon between his temporary jobs, helping out with everything from fixing loose hinges to peeling vegetables. Simon hoped that this year's Christmas Eve would hold a very different story to the last.

"Help yourself," he pointed to the cup of tea and newspaper on Bill's usual place by the radiator, as Bill reappeared freshly shaved and looking as if he were about to go on parade in his shined shoes and pressed trousers. The door opened and Simon looked up to see June and Pearl, on their way in.

"Morning dear," June called. She turned to her sister. "Show him, Pearl!"

With a self-important grin, Pearl held up a large cake tin. "I've been bakin'!" she shouted, although no one was more than two feet from her.

"Can I see?" Simon asked, taking the tin and carefully opening the lid. Inside was a neatly arranged selection of luridly iced fairy cakes. "They look tasty and such gorgeous colours; you must have worked very hard to make all these!" he exclaimed.

"June helped me," she beamed. Simon glanced at June, a neat, white-haired lady whose life was bound around that of her dependant sister. She was bursting with pride at Pearl's achievement. Pearl was an unexpected child, born to parents who were already in late middle-age. June was seventeen years old when they brought little Pearl home from the hospital and doted on her little sister from the minute they met. In those days, children like Pearl were often called feeble minded and parents were advised to leave their child in some soulless institution and forget about them. Not Pearl; her parents and sister cared for her, respected her differences, and resisted all the pressure to 'put her away.' Pearl had grown into a happy middle-aged lady herself now, and June was trying very hard to give her some independence.

"We'll leave you to it, Simon," June called, as the sisters walked towards the connecting door. "Back for a coffee after we've done the cleaning."

Bill stood up to help Simon, who was putting Harvest festival invitations in bundles to be delivered to local schools. As he did the door opened; it was Laura. She smiled as she shook off her wet coat.

"Hi, Bill. Weather's terrible, isn't it?"

He nodded, looked past her. "Where's 'littl'un?"

"School, making some strange thing out of pasta and egg boxes when I left!"

Bill smiled, and took the leaflets out of Simons hand, since he appeared to have forgotten the job in hand.

Laura turned towards Simon. Whenever he saw her, Simon's heart did a little skip. To call her his soulmate seemed unoriginal, but 'girlfriend' simply did her no justice. Tall and energetic, Laura's tough, no nonsense manner inspired confidence in most and occasionally caused offence to others. Only those close to her saw the fragile, uncertain girl behind the 'I've got it sorted' mask. He smiled to himself. She looked at him, enquiring. "What?"

"Nothing." he answered. "Just thinking." He looked into her eyes. "Coffee?"

It was her turn to laugh now. They had worked side by side for nearly three years and for at least the last two had spent as much time together outside of work as they could. They loved each other, there was no doubt about it, but who would be first to declare it? She did not dare. It had to come from him; declaring your love meant dealing with it. Some action would be needed. Best to leave things well alone. For now.

*****

A hundred miles away, in the office of her large salon, Simon's twin sister, Helen, was worried. On the desk in front of her was a pregnancy testing kit. She kept telling herself she was being ridiculous. They had been so careful; *she* had been so careful. And she was probably only a month late. Helen's periods had never had exactly clockwork timing. What with all the rushing about, her obsession with remaining a fit size zero, and the constant heavy workload, Helen could not pinpoint exactly how late she was. Or wasn't. The trouble was, she felt different. No morning sickness or huge bust…just different. And her face had changed; somehow her skin was different, softer maybe, her face rounder. Or was it just imagination? Her thoughts were going round in circles. Finally, she leapt from the chair, snatched up the kit and stamped into the bathroom.

*****

Later that evening, Simon made himself a cup of tea and walked softly down the tiny hallway to the lounge and seated himself in the worn armchair. He switched the TV on for the rugby match, just loud enough to hear. Too loud though, it seemed, as the familiar yodel travelled down the hallway.

"Siiiimon!"

"Go to sleep, sunshine."

"Are you watching the rugby?"

"I was." Simon walked to the bottom of the staircase, trying to keep one eye on the TV screen through the doorway.

"Did anyone get any tries yet?"

"I don't know."

"Why don't you know?"

"I don't know because I am standing here talking to you!"

"I'm thirsty."

"Then I'll bring you a drink and then it's time to sleep."

Simon took the cartoon character cup into Nicky's room. The child immediately sat up, alert and ready to chat forever. Laura had assured him that Nicky was sound asleep and that he would stay that way until morning. The trouble was, she said that last time, and the time before that. Nicky had a way of being out of bed and snuggled up on the arm chair with Simon, within half an hour of his mum leaving him in the care of his favourite babysitter. And that was how Laura found them when she returned from work later that night.

Six

Catherine maintained the same dull and pleasant façade which had held her together for so long. The constant anxiety had become so familiar it was like the ever-present buzz of the freezer, unnoticed. She knew, as she always did, that Graham would lose his infatuation with this latest fling, then things would return to normal. Today, at least, there was something to look forward to. She was to visit Floss. Since her transforming trip to London, Catherine had taken a more 'celebratory' approach to her curves. Today she wore the usual twinset, pearls and pleated skirt, but the twinset was in coral pink and the waist cinched with a wide belt. As soon as Graham had left for work, she hurried around, tidying up, then jumped in the car and sped away.

A glance up showed Bee's curtains were still closed. No need to feel bad, Catherine thought, relieved. She had directions to Floss' house and was there within the hour, ridiculously early. She had at least an hour to kill before she could decently arrive 'just a little early.' Floss was evidently lucky enough to live in the Gate House to Parlstone Hall, a very fine estate owned by some country aristocrat who, apparently, spent most of his time in London. The manor house was not visible from the road, the estate itself being surrounded by high red stone walls, overhung by wild-looking trees. Despite the feel of being deep in the countryside, the nearest town lay only two miles further along the road.

It was worth a look, Catherine thought, astounded at her adventurous spirit. The town was more like an overgrown village than a town. An upmarket village, stuffed with pubs, churches and antique shops. It was easy to find a parking space so early in the morning; most workers had left and schoolchildren were still being dropped at school. A few early risers were heading for the supermarket at the end of the street. A flower shop caught her eye, its buckets of colour and scent spilling out onto the pavement. Catherine chose a plentiful bouquet of purple and gold splashed with blood red roses. She looked at her watch, still plenty of time. She was expected at 11:30. Catherine surveyed the street again. Across the street, on the pavement opposite, stood a very smart-looking hair salon, 'Salon Maurice'. She had been meaning to do something about her hair for ages. The prices looked rather steep and she almost changed her mind, then Graham's voice replayed in her mind, "Busy, busy, busy…"

"Busy doing what, though?" she said to herself, bitterly. "I need cheering up!"

She pushed open the door. A bell clanged somewhere at the back of the shop, a rather stout balding man stepped smartly out from a door behind the sinks. His look was a question; she stammered out her request.

"I don't suppose you have any appointments available right now, do you?"

He smiled unexpectedly. "As a matter of fact, I do. A client just cancelled. Come and take a seat, madam. I am Maurice." He pronounced it 'Maureece,' and made a slight bow as she sat on the salon chair. Catherine was reminded of Hercule Poirot, which was probably not his intention.

Looking at her reflection, she wondered if all hairdressers' mirrors were designed to make you look as old, fat and tatty as possible. Perhaps they switched to the flattering mirror when you had your eyes closed for the hairspray at the end. A limp 'trainee' with hair an alarming shade of copper, was directed to put Catherine's flowers in water during the rather grandly named 'consultation'. Returning with a pile of gossip magazines and a glass of sparking water, the trainee placed them quickly on the bay in front of Catherine. Then dashed off towards the main desk to answer the phone. Maurice picked up a strand of hair in each hand and let it drop limply back to her shoulders.

"What did you have in mind?" he asked, as if a head transplant might be in order. The telephone shrilled again, Catherine was startled.

"Reception!" Maurice trumpeted. The same young girl loped to the phone and began to talk in hushed tones. Then louder:

"I'm afraid Maurice is with a client at the moment," she said, covering the mouthpiece and mouthing "Tamsin Fazakerley" at Catherine's stylist. He shook his head, emphatically spreading his hands in horror at the phone.

Charlene smiled, knowingly. "I'll just look at his bookings." She rustled the appointments book at the receiver. "I'm terribly sorry, Miss Fazakerley, but you *did* cancel and Maurice is fully booked all week. I could ask if he could squeeze you in first thing tomorrow…no…no afternoons at all, I'm afraid." She grimaced at Maurice, who was combing through Catherine's hair. "I'm sorry you feel that way, but Maurice really is a very popular stylist...Well, that's up to you, Miss…Yes…Yes. Thank you. Goodbye." She replaced the receiver.

Maurice met Catherine's eyes in the mirror. "Sorry about that," he smiled. "One of our more challenging customers!"

"I do understand," Catherine smiled in return. "My daughter runs a salon in Birmingham. She gets them all the time. I don't think she's quite as diplomatic as your young lady here, though."

They all laughed. Catherine having a daughter 'in the trade' put her relationship with Maurice and his junior on a new footing. Catherine was surprised to find that they had heard of Helen and that both salons had been regional finalists in some big National Styling Competition. Helen was most definitely a rising star in the hair artiste's firmament. Of course, her treatment from that moment was exceptional. Maurice promised to transform Catherine into a new woman, and in only one and a half hours. The experience was exhilarating, she was pampered and preened. They persuaded her to have a manicure 'on the house' and Maurice's skilled scissor-work took inches off her hair, pounds off her face and years off her age.

Whether it was the haircut or the way it made her feel did not matter. Catherine walked out of the place a different woman. She crossed the road heading for the car. Seeing a bakery whose windows were amply filled with plump cakes, she darted in and chose four of the most delicious looking confections which, when packed in their box, she carried carefully to the car. As she opened the door someone tapped her on her shoulder. Catherine turned around quickly. It was Floss, holding up a matching cake box.

"Snap!" she chimed, triumphantly. "You're looking great!"

"I was a little early," Catherine explained." Well, a lot early actually. I hate to be late! I had a mad moment and had a complete new look."

"I think it was a very sane moment, Catherine. It's so stylish and elegant. Maurice himself, I presume?"

Catherine nodded, pleased with her friend's reaction. "Where did you leave your car?"

"It's just around the corner. I'll meet you at my house, if you've finished shopping, that is."

Catherine looked down at the flowers and cakes as if she'd never seen them before. "Oh, shopping! Of course! These are for you." She handed her gifts over to their intended recipient. "I'll meet you at your place."

Floss' home was, as Catherine had guessed, the old gatekeeper's cottage. Inside, the bittersweet combination of roses and cigar smoke hung in the air. Each room seemed stuffed with colour and comfort, every corner imbued with humour and good taste. A lifetime's memorabilia scattered through the place appeared neither haphazard, nor deliberate. Poised precariously between a clutter and a collection, Floss' home abundantly reflected the character of its owner.

"What a beautiful home." Catherine followed her friend into the kitchen. They talked of pleasant things as Floss arranged her flowers. After a while, Catherine, unused to watching another at work, asked if she could be useful in any way.

"Preparing lunch, anything at all," she said. "There must be something I can do?"

"Everything's pretty much in hand, really," Floss assured her, "but if you wouldn't mind putting our cakes on a plate, you'll find one in the bottom cupboard there."

She nodded her head in the direction of the vast Georgian sideboard. Catherine found a serving plate and began to arrange the cakes, remarking at the beauty of the china ware. Floss informed her that the whole set was a gift from Andrew, one of his 'finds' at an auction. As they chatted, Catherine marvelled to herself at the familiarity of their friendship. She felt at home. She was surprised to find herself thinking of Andrew. The dangerous thought was quickly cast out by the request for further help. As Floss continued to cut and place the flowers, Catherine pulled various cling-wrapped dishes from the fridge and began to make a pot of tea.

"There!" Floss exclaimed, standing back to admire her completed arrangement.

Catherine looked up from her corner of the kitchen to see a fanfare of shape and colour. Floss had added trails of ivy to the tall vase. The once formal bouquet had become a wild, tumbling cascade of nature.

"It's breathtaking!" Catherine was genuinely filled with admiration. "You're gifted, Floss. Really!"

Floss smiled. "Thank you," she grinned. "I can't abide false modesty, my dear, so I'll just accept your plaudits with good grace." They both laughed loudly. "I'll just clear up this mess, and we'll have lunch."

Catherine helped to gather up all the floral detritus which spread across the worktops and floor. As the stems and scraps were thrown away, Floss said, "Grab a tray, we'll eat in comfort, in the sitting room." The sitting room was indeed a picture of comfort. A fire roaring in the grate, threw golden light across the long chestnut coffee table that lay in front of it between two overstuffed sofas. Catherine, following Floss' lead, placed the laden tray on the table. Once filled with all Floss had prepared, the ladies' lunch for two resembled an afternoon tea for six hearty eaters.

"I may have over catered" Floss stated, rather unnecessarily.

There was a knock on the door, followed immediately by the figure of Andrew bursting in, closely followed by two muddy golden Labradors who headed straight for the food. Amid frantic cries of "Amber, Buster, heel!" and "Oh, Buster, no!" Catherine, immediately realising the threat to their mid-day feast, managed to grab one dog by the collar. The other though, younger and more determined, helped himself joyfully to as much as he could in the few precious seconds of freedom. Finally, no longer able to ignore Andrew's command to come to heel, the Labradors, looking both guilty and penitent turned to look at Andrew.

"It's no good trying to look sorry," Andrew said, "when your tail is wagging!"

Floss, not at all pleased that the cosy tete-a-tete she had hoped for was now in chaos, snapped, "Oh, for goodness sake, Andrew, take those dogs out of here!" gathering the scattered sandwiches and everything else Buster had touched onto one plate, she thrust it at him "And you might as well throw this lot in the bin!"

Andrew did as he was told, while Catherine and Floss surveyed the damage. Having secured the dogs in the utility room, Andrew returned, apologising for his rather spectacular and unexpected interruption to their day. He had been passing, he explained, and thought he would call in. "I should have called ahead," he said. "I'm sorry."

Floss, who could never stay cross with anyone for long, least of all her beloved brother-in-law, said he might as well join them, since it was lunchtime.

"I don't want to disrupt your plans any more than I already have," Andrew said, looking hopefully at both ladies. "I really am sorry…"

"There is still enough here to feed an army," Catherine laughed, passing him a plate, "so no harm done."

"You will learn, Catherine, if you haven't already," Andrew smiled, as he piled it high with sandwiches, scones and cheese straws, "that Floss lives by the maxim 'Food is Love.'"

Floss laughed, "I can't deny it," she said, offering Catherine a dish loaded with three varieties of savoury tarts. Catherine looked at Andrew, and shrugged, helplessly as the three of them roared with laughter.

The room was cosy; the lunch delicious; the company delightful. The relaxed, rational, informed conversation, in sharp contrast to the shallow prejudiced prattle of her usual circle, was as refreshing to Catherine as the freshly-made coffee which completed her meal.

Catherine dabbed at her mouth with the linen napkin and leaned back contentedly in her chair.

"You look happy," Andrew remarked.

"I am thoroughly spoilt," Catherine purred, eyes closed.

"You thoroughly deserve it!" Floss remarked. "Now, if you don't object, I shall indulge one of my few and minor vices." She held up a Panatela cigar.

"Go ahead, please," Catherine nodded.

Dangerously close to nodding off, Catherine forced her eyes open and looked up at the large stone mantel piece. To her amazement, there in the corner sat two Toby jugs, identical in all but size to the one she had just put up to auction.

"Martha Gunn!" she exclaimed.

Floss was astounded. "You're absolutely right!" After a pause, glancing quickly at Andrew, she continued, "She's not very well known. Are you a collector?"

"Not at all," Catherine answered. "I saw one once and found out a bit about it. I was told they were very rare, though."

"And so they are." Andrew said. "This set in particular, if complete, is the only one known to exist. These two, with their matching third, were apparently presented to the real Martha in her old age, as a sort of thank you from the people of her town. She was quite a celebrity in her day you know."

"How exciting, Floss" Catherine said. "How did you come to have these two?"

"Martha had a distant connection to the Starling family," Floss answered, looking again at Andrew, who continued the story.

"The complete set was passed down through the family for years. Then, between the wars, the old gent who owned them died, leaving one jug to each of his three daughters. Our great, great grandmother got the middle sized one; we found the bigger one about twenty years ago in America. We've never been able to trace the little one to this day."

"They must be very valuable" Catherine said.

"Oh! No doubt about it. If we had the set it would be phenomenal. But I'd never sell. Aside from the fact that it's family history, I actually like dear Martha. She was a formidable woman. I couldn't bear to part with her," completed Floss.

An idea had been forming in Catherine's mind. Floss' words precipitated the deed. Within the hour Catherine had made her goodbyes and left.

Floss returned to the sitting room where Andrew sat thoughtfully, his long legs stretched out towards the fire, both dogs sleeping soundly at his feet. She looked at him seriously and he returned her gaze, equally serious. The unspoken dilemma hanging heavily between them. Andrew spoke first. "I know," he said, "I know, but maybe if I just wait, hope and pray…"

Florence shook her head in wide-eyed exasperation. Andrew had been waiting, hoping and praying for the right woman for nearly twenty years. There had been a couple of near misses early on and, more recently, two disastrous years of cohabitation with an actress in the United States, who was as greedily unwholesome on the inside as she was sweet and decent on the surface. Floss' own heart had nearly broken at his devastation and his determination to remain safely alone for the rest of his life.

"One way or another, Andrew," she sighed, "you'd better pray for a miracle"

*****

It was hot in the church kitchen. They were preparing shepherd's pie and apple crumble for the weekly pensioner's lunch. Simon chopped apples, while Bill, an excellent cook, put the finishing touches to the last pie. Through the serving hatch in the main hall, Simon could hear Reverend Tim practicing 'We all live in a Yellow Submarine' on the old piano, while June and Pearl were laying the tables, putting out carefully folded paper napkins on each plastic table top, along with cutlery and condiments. Despite the heat, Bill's shirt remained buttoned to the top and his tie knotted neatly in place.

"I have something I wish to say to you, Padre," Bill said solemnly, as he pushed the last pie into the oversized oven and closed the door on it.

Simon stopped his apple chopping at once. Bill was a man of few words. But when he chose to speak, it was well worth listening.

"Yes, Bill."

"It's about that young Laura and her lad."

"Yes, Bill."

Reverend Tim came to the end of his chorus as Bill continued, "I want to know your intentions."

"My intentions, I…well…in what way…I don't know what you…?"

"I think you know very well what I am talking about. That young lad thinks the world of you, and so do we all"

Simon looked round up as there was a sudden lull in the clatter from the hall. Reverend Tim had turned on his piano stool and was looking at the hatch as if it were a TV screen, June and Pearl were evidently very interested in the conversation and straining to hear every word. June caught Simon's eye and looked away, embarrassed. Pearl just stood there, arms folded, waiting for the next instalment. Simon smiled at her.

"Are you lot in on this as well then?" he asked. "Only I don't think it's fair if you are all going to gang up on me!"

"Oh! It's not like that!" flustered June.

"No, not at all, just ..." faltered Reverend Tim, simultaneously.

There was a pause as they both waited for the other to speak. Pearl took the opportunity while she had it. "We all think you should marry Laura, only Laura is too shy, and you are too shy, so Bill is going to bang your heads together!" She announced with a triumphant nod.

Silence filled the hall; the half-peeled apple in Simon's hand began to turn a little brown around the edges. He looked around the little gang of misfits…who were as dear to him as his own family.

He raised his hands in surrender, "I suppose I'd better ask her then!"

******

An hour after her mysterious flight from Floss' home, Catherine was in Westbury's auction rooms, withdrawing her Toby jug from the sale. There was some commotion as Mr Phillips emerged from his room to investigate her unusual decision. Was she unhappy with their valuation? Had she received a private offer? To this last, Catherine responded with a smile. In a way, she had. The jug would go home to a place where she was truly valued.

"I find I just can't part with her to a stranger," she explained. "I have found her a home myself. I am sorry for your trouble; I simply must have her back."

"Of course," soothed Mr Phillips, "but you may like to know there is a strong chance that it will fetch an even higher price than we discussed."

"You mean you have a buyer already?"

"Let's say we are aware of one particularly interested collector. He wouldn't let himself be easily outbid."

"Well, I'm sorry to disappoint you, gentlemen, really I am, but I have had an offer I can't refuse."

After some further discussion and form filling, Catherine was handed her little package and set off for the old Gate House for the second time that day.

Seven

A late lunch for Graham was ostensibly to discuss marketing and sales strategies with his management team and the directors. Graham saw it only as a means to impress Mandy. His skilled deferential 'mateyness' towards the higher management, from whose lower echelons he hoped soon to ascend, was faintly amusing to Mandy. She watched them lap it up like pigs at a trough. She was detached, observant, and sharply aware of his fine honed skill. He was not obsequious, not desperate, not after their jobs; yet all three were there, masked by his charming, guileless exterior. His off-the-cuff remarks were carefully prepared, his confidences universal. As Graham built his apprentice piece, Mandy looked on with the easy confidence of a master craftsman.

After lunch, she allowed him to drive her back to the office, with only the two of them in the car. The ten-minute journey was farcical. In his desperate attempt to impress, he talked and talked. The more he spoke, the more she withdrew. He heard himself laughing too loudly at his feeble humour and embarrassed himself with his own schoolboy innuendo. As he pulled into his parking space and turned off the engine, he sighed loudly.

"What's up, Mandy, have you taken a vow of silence?"

She smiled as she uncoiled from the car. "You talk too much, Graham. You would learn a lot if you listened to people."

With that she strode towards the door of the massive hi-tech building, paying little attention to Graham who hurried to catch up. He was incensed when, as they reached the lifts, she quickly slipped in as the door was closing, leaving him stranded once more.

"That's it," he told himself. "She's over."

Graham was foul-mouthed and foul-tempered for the remainder of the day. At around 6:00pm he was loudly berating his secretary, for the third or fourth time that afternoon, when Mandy popped her head around his office door.

"Sorry to interrupt, Mr Chandler. Can you spare a minute when you're finished?" He glared at her. Mandy looked at the secretary as if unaware.

"My goodness, Mrs Marchment, are you still here? We don't deserve you. Don't you normally finish at 5:30?"

She replied quietly, "I'm paid until 5:00 pm, actually."

"Your family will wonder where you are. Can't you let this poor woman go home, Mr Chandler?" She winked confidentially at the grateful secretary.

Mr Chandler had been in 'one of his moods' for most of the day. Most days he was charming in a faintly slimy, patronising way, but there were times when he was unbearable. Miss Belton seemed to be handling him well, though, Mrs Marchment thought. Everyone knew she was the latest in his long, long line of 'victims.' Silly girls, thinking a few nights in his bed would guarantee a long-term romance, or a step up the career ladder. Most of them only lasted a few weeks. She never warned them. No point; they would more than likely go ahead with it any way, and she'd be the baddie of the piece. At least this way there was someone to pick up the pieces afterwards. And arrange the paperwork when they requested a transfer. She looked at him. His eyes were locked on Miss Belton's. Mrs Marchment coughed, pulling him back from whatever fantasy he had locked into. His eyes turned to her. He scowled. Sighed. Then waved her away impatiently.

"Yes, yes, of course. You must go home, Mrs Marchment. God forbid you should do a little overtime. Go home. Go home."

The loyal secretary was stung. Even Mandy was surprised at his acrimony. She watched as the woman turned and left, her expression speaking her anger. Graham noticed nothing since he was still hitting the keyboard with unnecessary ferocity, then throwing papers into his open briefcase. As the door closed the two were silent. Graham continued to 'work.' Mandy faced him, waiting. Graham was expecting some sort of flirtatious, apologetic approach from her. Then he would tell her it was too late; she would cry; he would relent. Maybe. He wanted to conquer her. To his surprise, she stood in silence.

"Well!" he barked, still looking at the computer screen. "You wanted to see me. What is it?"

"Don't worry," she chirped, brightly. "You're obviously very busy." She left, closing the door quietly behind her.

He finally looked up from the mindless, unimportant figures he had been bashing into his computer. Incredibly, she had gone. He leapt from the chair almost, hurdling across the desk, and lunged through the door in one movement.

"Mandy!" he cried.

His office was one of six which opened onto an open plan area, filled with lesser managers and their secretaries. He realised, as his desperate yell hit the far wall, that some eager to impress stragglers were still at their desks. He felt rather than saw their collective smirk. Returning to the safety of his office, he grabbed his case and suit jacket, then walked as calmly as he could towards the exit and the lifts. It was pure instinct. He was in pursuit. He had no plan, no thought at all in his mind but catching up with Mandy. The lift opened. He flew out, almost falling over his own feet in his haste. There she was, cool, assured, chatting pleasantly with the security guard.

She turned and smiled. "Finished at last! You work too hard, Mr Chandler. Doesn't he?" She had evidently decided to drag the unsuspecting security guard into her scheme. The man nodded, looked expressively at his colleague. He had been with the building for many years. He had seen it all so many times before.

"Yes, Miss," he agreed. "Much too hard."

She looked into Graham's face. "I'll walk you to your car."

As the pair left, not quite arm in arm, the security guard turned again to his colleague.

"Hormones," he said.

*****

Floss had not long said goodbye to Andrew and settled herself into her customary chair for a snooze when the doorbell clanged her awake. Surprised and delighted, she found Catherine waiting at the door. "Come in! Come in!" She waved her friend inside. "I'll put the kettle on."

Catherine remained on the doorstep. "You must wonder why I dashed off so quickly after lunch."

112

Catherine said, looking past Floss into the hallway and sitting room beyond.

Floss, smiled "He's already left" she said. Thinking Catherine had come back to apologise for her sudden departure, Floss begged her not to worry, and again offered to make tea. Catherine seemed rather agitated. "No, thank you. I have to get home before Graham does, or...well...the thing is..." She found herself getting tongue tied. She took a deep breath.

"It's...I'd like you to have this. I know you'll care for it. I'm so glad I realised before... well, here it is anyway. Must dash. See you soon." She pecked a very bewildered Floss on the cheek, climbed back into the car and sped home.

Floss took the supermarket carrier bag into her lounge. Inside was a cardboard box. It looked like a large dice. The box was heavily taped and marked fragile. Carefully, she took a pair of nail scissors to the tape. The box opened to reveal, shrouded in shredded paper, the missing Martha Gunn jug. Floss sat down, shocked.

"After all this time," she whispered to herself. "Home again."

She placed the Toby jug carefully with its mates. The completed set looked splendid, reunited at last. Floss smiled. "Catherine, my dear! Whatever next?"

*****

As the pensioners scraped the last of their crumble from the green china plates, Bill, Pearl and June were up to their elbows in soapy water. Reverend Tim and Simon cleared the last of the tables and handed round cups of tea and coffee. The door opened and, as usual, in flew Nicky, with Laura a few paces behind, loaded with coat, PE kit, backpack and lunch box.

"Pearl! Pearl!" he shouted through the serving hatch "Did you save me a pudding?"

Beaming, Pearl put a huge scoop of ice cream on the equally huge portion of crumble she had saved for him. "Sit down nicely and I'll bring it to you," she said.

"Woah! Thanks, Pearl!" The boy ate as only a small boy just back from school can eat.

Pearl looked at Bill and June, who had emerged from the Kitchen, drying their hands. She looked at Simon. "We'll be going, then!" she piped. Simon looked horrified. "No time like the present!" she continued, regardless.

"Pearl!" chided June.

The whole place fell silent. Everyone looked at Simon, including Laura, who was beginning to wonder what was going on. Pearl put her hands on her hips and nodded, first at Simon, then at Laura … "Go on then!" she said in a stage whisper.

Simon swallowed hard and looked at Laura.

"What is it?" she asked.

"Well, I have been wanting to say this for some time, but, well, this isn't exactly as I had planned... neither the time nor the place... however..."

"Her-humm!" Pearl coughed loudly.

"Okay. Well. Laura..." Suddenly resolute, he crossed the floor, and amidst all the half-cleared tables and the bemused and cheering pensioners, Simon Chandler got down on one knee, took Laura's hand, and asked nervously, "Laura, I love you, will you marry me?"

*****

Catherine's exhilaration lasted until she pulled into her drive. Bee, lying in wait, pounced from her side of the fence as Catherine arrived. "You'll be pleased to hear I'm thinking of cancelling our Saturday Supper," she drawled, triumphantly. "Roger can't get home from Manchester until tomorrow night, too late to go out." The truth was that Roger had said he did not want to go out, he had insisted she cancel. Which was unusual and she had agreed.

"Why should I be pleased, Bee?" Catherine sighed, preparing for one of Bee's 'poor old me' onslaughts. "I enjoy our get-togethers."

"Seems to me you've got something else to interest you now. I was useful enough 'til you met your common little catering friend."

Catherine was taken aback at Bee's remark, venomous even for Bee. She must have looked shocked. Bee's gaze searched for pain, and was surprised to find impatience, even amusement there.

"Don't look so surprised, Cath, we used to go everywhere together, now you're off on secret missions all over the place."

Catherine apologised. She had not intended to hurt her friend's feelings. She could not help but feel disloyal. Which was exactly the effect Bee hoped to produce. Catherine apologised again.

"I really am sorry Bee. I'll try to make it up to you. Perhaps we could go out one day next week."

"Better than that!" Bee exclaimed, finding herself at exactly the point she had aimed for. "Let's go to the Cholmondeley Park antiques market, tomorrow."

It was Bee's turn to look shocked, as indeed she was, when Catherine explained that she was to attend the very same event with her 'common caterer' and, even more shocking, as a common caterer's apprentice! "I'll be glad to give you a lift," she offered, "but it's a very early start and we won't pack up before five. So, in a way, cancelling the meal tomorrow will make life a lot easier for me."

Bees eyes narrowed, Catherine was momentarily saved the full force of Bee's wrath by the arrival of Graham's car, sweeping into the drive. What remained of Catherine's bravura seeped slowly into the paving stones. Her secret was out. She hadn't planned to tell him this way, now Bee would maliciously spew out her plans before she was ready. His meal wasn't ready; there was no ice in the freezer. As Graham slammed his door and strode towards them, she felt like a rabbit between two hungry foxes.

"Hi, there, sexy!" Graham leaned across his wife to embrace Bee, who glared at Catherine.

"Darling, rotten old Roger is working and won't be home until tomorrow night, so I'm afraid our meal will have to be a little later tomorrow."

"Scared I'll beat him on the golf course again, no doubt," joked Graham. He saw an advantage. "As it happens, I have to work tomorrow any way; we're moving the office around. Only opportunity there is, I'm afraid, but you girls will still be able to shop, no doubt." He laughed, then saw the women's faces, Catherine doubtful, Bee sour. His smile locked; he looked at Bee for an explanation.

Bee looked at her. She could almost be a spiteful little nine-year-old at school. 'I'm going to tell!' her face said, 'I'm going to tell!' *Here it comes*, thought Catherine.

"Catherine's much, much too busy to waste time with me on a Saturday, Graham!"

He looked at Catherine, spoke to Bee. "Meaning?"

"Oh, hasn't she told you yet? I expect it was to be a surprise." Her tone was sarcastic, mocking.

Graham knew he was about to be angry, his colour rose. He waited for the crescendo, Bee's words massaging his rage. Slowly, skilfully she brought him to the peak of anticipation. "Far too busy... surely not behind your back...something to hide... always said you wouldn't allow her to work..." It was almost pleasure; he wallowed in her acid words which became indistinct with his rage.

His voice was tight, straining. "Tell me!" he grated.

Catherine opened her mouth to speak. Bee finished it.

"She won't be shopping, Graham; your wife will be serving hot dogs from a mobile caff!"

"No!" He shuddered, snarling.

Bee dashed her hands together, the job done. Graham almost gnashed his teeth in disapproval.

Catherine swayed both physically and mentally then got herself back on a firm footing. "Well, if I don't go, I could come to work with you and help out with the office move..."

"Don't be bloody ridiculous!" he shouted in alarm. "Do what you want. I don't care!"

"I'll see you later." Bee danced away, leaving Catherine to mop up all the hostility she had left behind. Not wanting a scene in front of the neighbours,

Catherine hurried into the house. Inside, Graham pinned her against the wall.

"You stupid cow!" he shouted, nose to nose. Then, releasing her, "Do what you want! I'm going out!"

He left her, empty, breathless and afraid. She slid down the wall and wept.

*****

Helen turned, reaching for the screaming alarm clock, switching it off and pulling it to her. He was sleeping deeply beside her...she was glad he had not woken. She walked into the shower. Standing under the steamy water, she tried to make sense of her situation, a predicament that no amount of wishing or wisdom could wash away. Strangely, she had always been so sure of what she would do...until it happened. And it had to happen with *this* man. Of the few affairs she had had, the inconvenient consequence of this one should have been dealt with simply and quickly. She would not even need more than a couple of days off work. He would have been none the wiser, and...but that was the problem. She did not want to deceive him, she did not want to exclude him, and more than anything she did not want to destroy his child. Unaware, she stroked her stomach... then, taking a deep breath, she shook off her thoughts, wrapped herself in a towel and joined him in the bedroom once more. He smiled up at her.

"Take a sicky," he pleaded, smiling, as she applied her make up.

"Sadly, I can't," she answered, "since I am the boss!" She turned her back to the dressing table mirror. "Anyway, the vampire's expecting you!"

"Don't!" He fell back onto the pillows in mock horror.

She looked at him, the laugh in her eyes turning to sadness. She turned back to the mirror. He climbed from the bed and stood behind her, returning her gaze.

There were tears in Helen's eyes. He had made her cry. "I'm so sorry" he whispered. "Helen, it's just so…"

She began to apply her make up, smiling at him. "Don't you worry," she said," I'm just being silly"

He dressed quickly. "I could just tell her, leave it all behind," he said, with little certainty.

"You'll never do it," she looked up at him, "and I can't expect you to."

"Things were never meant to get this…complicated." He looked away, ashamed, kissed her on the cheek and left in a hurry. She met her own eyes in the mirror.

"Complicated it certainly is," she told herself.

Eight

Catherine woke early, intending to slip out without waking Graham. His side of the bed was unruffled. He had not even bothered to pretend. This was not fair. This was not playing the game. Until now they had always had a sort of understanding. He pretended it was not happening. She pretended to be deceived. There was a perverse unity in their contract of denial. She looked in the mirror as she brushed her teeth.

"It's not happening," she told herself. "I can cope."

She spat out the bitter taste of betrayal with her toothpaste. Somehow, she managed to push the pain away, swallowing it with her coffee. She could not eat.

*****

Laura was having second thoughts. She knew she loved Simon, and Nicky thought the world of him. She knew the chance of a new life, a fresh start, was more than she had ever hoped for. But she could not quite believe that Simon really knew his own feelings. Besides, he was very well thought of, not just by the people of St Christopher's, but by the people who funded the organisation. And how could a man married to a woman like her ever get the respect he deserved? Laura had come from a good, if strict, home in a small village in Dorset. Life was boring if you were an outgoing, creative teenager, and Laura soon found herself with the wrong crowd. Despite her parent's protests, Laura, at sixteen, set up home with a lad not much older than herself who she met at a festival. It had not occurred to her to wonder how this 18-year-old had a flat, a car and plenty of money when most of their peers were still living with their parents. When she found out he was selling pills and more to her school friends at parties, she told herself no one was forcing them to buy the stuff, after all, she never touched it. She liked the feeling of being one of the gang. He said he would love her forever, but eventually only used her as punching bag.

Ashamed, she finally ran away, but not to her parents, who, she had not realised, would have welcomed her, but the furthest she could get on the money she had. It was not far, but it was far enough. She lived rough, from hand to mouth. The man she had escaped had left her with little money, but it was not long before she realised, he had left her with a lasting memento. Nicky. And it was Nicky who had changed her life. A tiny perfect baby. Who would ever have thought that something so good could result from something so very bad?

With Nicky to care for, Laura returned home and was surprised to find her strict, traditional parents were only concerned that she had been away for so long. They welcomed Nicky with literally open arms and settled Laura back into their home as if she had never been gone. When Nicky was two, Laura moved north, to study part time at university and work at the St Christopher's House there. And that is how she had ended up engaged to the best man in the world, and sitting on the bed crying as she called her parents to tell them.

*****

In the early morning, Mandy slipped out of bed; she looked down at Graham. He was good looking. In sleep, the lines and creases in his usually animated face deepened. He looked older, careworn, maybe. She felt a fleeting rush of compassion, swiftly dissolving. For a moment, she thought she might be falling in love. She sighed softly in relief. She had to be in control.

Mandy was well aware of her lover's reputation. She was determined that she would be the one to win him from the silly lump of a wife he always went back to. It was a matter of pride; she was driven purely by the need to win. Graham was easily attainable on his terms; any girl with a reasonable figure and flirtatious manner would soon find themselves dining with him at some hotel, and eventually waking up with him in the executive suite, impressed, flattered, and disposable.

Mandy played to win. Her way. She could almost imagine herself in love, if needs be. Graham turning up unexpectedly last night had moved things on a little faster than she had planned. He had been furious, seething with rage. His silly wife had some inappropriate friend or something. She could not understand his objection to the woman making plans and friends of her own, particularly since he was evidently so disinterested in all that his wife did. However, his swollen sense of social pride and status had been dealt a great blow.

Mandy soothed him. She had been careful not to denigrate his wife or to say anything which would obviously build herself up at his wife's expense. Mandy had, however, brought him a very good wine in an expensive crystal goblet. She sat him in the stylish plum leather armchair, facing the pair of expensive modern prints on the silk-covered wall. She had tutted, concurred, and "Oh no'd," in all the right places. When his rage had subsided, she had brought him baked salmon with Greek salad and warm bread. More wine, more talk, and they had gone to bed. Graham subdued; Mandy triumphant. It was their first night together and they had not made love.

Now it was morning; she turned and went into the bathroom. She poured an expensive lotion into the running water. Bubbles frothed and filled the tub. Mandy applied a little discreet make up, combed her hair into a tumble-down ponytail and fixed it with a golden clip. She slid into the scented foam, laid back and waited, the suspicion of a smile on her face.

*****

Catherine drove automatically to keep her appointment with Floss. Her sense of duty was once again overriding her true inclination. All she wanted was to hide; instead she slapped on a smile and forced the truth away. All the delicious anticipation, like a child waiting for Christmas day, had disappeared along with the dearly held delusions about her marriage. Setting up the stall, Catherine was so distracted she was almost withdrawn.

"Is something wrong?" Floss asked. "Is it Martha? She is yours really, you know."

Pulled from her thoughts by the idea that Floss may feel her friend was regretting yesterday's hasty gift. Catherine assured her that everything was perfectly fine.

"I'm glad to hear it" Floss breathed a sigh of relief. "When you didn't answer my text, I thought you'd had a change of mind, and I wouldn't blame you at all if you had. Martha, even on her own, is a very valuable piece."

Catherine pulled her phone from her pocket; she hadn't looked at it since yesterday. She read the tender message of thanks that Floss had sent. The kind words were almost too much to bear after the cruelty of last night. A tear slipped down her face. Catherine turned away. "Martha is where she belongs, Floss," she said, wiping the tear away, "I am very happy that you have her home at last." Catherine turned away and busied herself folding tea towels and trying to draw back her escaping tears

Floss noticed, of course, but the opportunity to talk about anything other than the task in hand just never came. Floss considered the patient approach to be the best. Catherine would tell what she wanted in her own time.

Meanwhile, the satisfaction of working with each other grew as they both realised that they formed a natural team. Catherine had an easy, quiet way with people, friendly and efficient. Compared to the usual brooding teenagers Floss recruited, Catherine was a godsend. She did not have to be asked to wipe off the preparation areas or to clear and clean the tables. She noticed when the ketchup was getting low and refilled it. She asked the customers if they liked the coffee strong or weak.

"You sure you haven't done this before?" Floss joked. "You're a natural!"

"Must be all those years at the kitchen sink!" They laughed together.

*****

As his wife was buttering bread rolls and slicing tomatoes, Graham woke in Mandy's bed. The air was moist with steam breathed from the bathroom, faintly scented, an invitation? He rose naked from the bed and pushed open the bathroom door.

"Do come in," she said. It was a rebuke.

"Sorry." He stumbled, "I should have knocked."

She looked beautiful, as she had planned to look. She glanced up at him. Instinctively he grabbed a towel and covered himself up.

"Thank you." She smiled. He felt rewarded.

"There's coffee made in the kitchen," she sighed, languid. The command hung between them. She knew the importance of this moment.

"I'll bring you a cup, darling," he said, eager to please. "Do you like to read the papers too?"

"As a rule!" she called as he hurried away to fetch what she wanted. She grinned to herself, softly sighing, "And I make the rules!"

*****

Laura mopped the floors of the St Christopher's House kitchen and hall. Baby clinic had just finished; all the mums and toddlers had gone, and there was just time for a cup of tea and a sandwich before the delivery of groceries from local collection points arrived. It would take all afternoon to sort them ready for the Harvest Festival tomorrow. She looked up from slicing cheese for her lunch as the door opened. It was Simon.

"Just in time for a cheese sandwich," she laughed. "How do you do it?" They settled down together at the small table in the window.

"A quick bite," he said, kissing her lightly on the cheek, "and then we are off to the shops!"

"We are? And what about the food that needs sorting for tomorrow?"

"It won't take long and I want to make an honest fiancée out of you!" Simon took an envelope of cash from his pocket. Laura stepped back, astonished.

"Where did you come by that?"

"Don't worry," he laughed. "I haven't robbed the church coffers. I've been saving for a rainy day. And as it happens, this is a perfectly sunny one."

They chatted, holding hands as they ate their lunch, when suddenly the door burst open. It was June, shaking, tearful, speechless. Simon and Laura jumped from their seats and put their arms around her, leading her to the sofa. For a few minutes they could get no sense out of her at all, except that it had something to do with

Pearl. Once they had found out that Pearl was in no immediate danger, not in hospital and not lost, they waited and listened as June told her story.

Pearl, it seemed, had a burning desire to own a special set of cake tins in the shape of a star. The only problem was, she had not enough money to buy one. Her funds were limited and she had always been taught to budget, spending money, after bills, was limited to £30 in any one week. Undaunted, Pearl had applied by telephone for instant free cash, as advertised on TV, for only £45. Of course, Pearl had never been overdrawn and never had a loan. So the loan was granted, and Pearl got her cash and went off to the cooking shop to buy her cake tins. The problem was that now the company were after her to pay back the loan - with vast interest.

"Exactly how much does she owe?" asked Simon.

June buried her head in her hands. "It's almost £500! It's impossible!"

Laura and Simon caught their breath; it was an enormous amount for June and Pearl to find in a hurry.

June wept. "It might as well be £5,000. It would be just as easy to get hold of! They will take Pearl away and put her in prison, or worse, in a home. They'll say I cannot look after her, or she cannot be responsible…Oh Pearl, Pearl, what shall I do?"

Simon looked at Laura, the same thought had occurred to them both. Laura gave a tiny nod and smiled

"June," said Simon, "I hope it's not £5,000 as we only have £500…"

June looked up, "I can't take your money!" she said. "No, I won't."

"Well, that's the whole point," said Laura, "it's not our money. An anonymous benefactor left this in the office today. They said they wanted it to be used for good. Please take it, June…for Pearl."

It was as if the sun had risen over the little church. June beamed. She took the envelope of cash.

"Thank you both," she said. "Thank you, Father God! Oh…and," she looked up, "God bless the anonymous benefactor!"

*****

Roger had been driving home for hours, it seemed, or maybe less than an hour, rolling past the same scenery that filled so many of his days. Time stretched out like an elastic band. He seemed to travel such a long, long way only to find that every day and every employee and every office was the same. Even the radio churned out the same mix of tired banter and well-worn songs. Being part of the corporate machine, with all the compromises and commercial trickery it entailed, had sucked the soul out of him.

Roger arrived home as Bee climbed out of the taxi, pulling her many useless purchases after her. As the driver pulled away, she ran across to him and kissed his cheek. He pulled away, unnoticed by a Bee absorbed in her troubles. She was in full flow, complaining, extolling, describing, on and on and on she talked, mindlessly repeating the same phrases over and over. The words wound uselessly around them. The less he appeared to listen, the more she repeated herself. Automatically he picked up her many packages and carried them to the house. He looked at Bee, as he followed her. Everything about her was sharp, angular. Her bony shoulder blades worked beneath her skimpy top as she struggled to unlock the door. Her profile was sharp, her high defined cheekbones highlighted with some unsubtle cosmetic. And the voice! Sharp, sharp, sharp.

"Roger! Wake up!" He was jolted from his reverie of disenchantment.

"Sorry, I'm tired."

"Well, we're out with the Chandlers tonight, it was too late to cancel and I didn't want to let everyone down. So you'd better perk up."

He dropped all her bags on the table.

"Bee, the last thing I need now is an evening with Mr Pretentious and poor old Catherine."

She turned on him, spite glittering in her eyes. He stood, impassive as she recited the 'I'm trapped here all week' litany. When she had finished, he looked her in the eye. She waited for an argument. Roger had begun to disagree with her more and more often over the last year. She had responded by redoubling her efforts to transform the interior of the house and the exterior of herself. That the cause of his discontent could lay any deeper was beyond her understanding. She glowered back at him. Triumphant, his silence meant he would apologise. He stared back, taking in her features. He noticed, as if for the first time, the deep lines around her mouth; the slight sagging of the skin beneath her chin. She had become mean, petulant, and it was written on her face. He felt sad. He missed what she used to be. He saw what she was, and in that moment became free of her.

"Okay," he said, and left the room.

*****

As the afternoon drew out, most stallholders were packing away, except the inexperienced, die-hard few, holding out in the hopes of making a sale to the last few stragglers who were wandering around the market. Floss called to Catherine who was wiping down the tables.

"Time to start packing away! Oh, I see you've already started. I'll be with you in a second."

She pulled down the corrugated shutter which closed the counter, turned everything off inside and joined Catherine in folding chairs and tables.

"Thanks so much for stepping in at the last minute, Catherine," she smiled. "You've no idea what a help it's been."

"Don't thank me, please," her friend replied. "I really have enjoyed it, more than I thought I would, actually."

"Me too," Floss laughed. "We work so well together. Not that young Kelly doesn't work hard, bless her, but she's only a kid. If I don't tell her exactly what to do, it doesn't get done."

Just then a stall holder came up to the café, and seeing it closed up, began to walk away. To Floss' surprise, Catherine called out to him.

"Everything alright, Arthur?"

He called back, "Yes, thanks. Just fancied a last cuppa. I'll get here earlier next time."

Catherine looked at Floss. "We've still got some hot water, haven't we?" Floss nodded. Catherine beckoned Arthur over. "I can make you a coffee if that's alright."

Of course it was alright. Arthur was delighted with his coffee, and Floss was delighted with Catherine.

"That's exactly what I mean," she said when the happy man had returned to his stall. "Customer service personified."

"Insurance, actually," Catherine smiled. "He bought breakfast, lunch and tea from us. Just making sure he does the same next time!"

"My point, exactly," said Floss.

*****

Graham had returned by the time Catherine arrived home. Nothing was said. Her silence disturbed him. Not reproachful. Not even resigned. This time it was different. She had become somehow self-contained. Her state of mind was hard to discern. He was relieved; he had no excuses to offer now, and she did not seem to want any. Of course, he did not comment on her late arrival, or taunt her about her day. He had to be content with not mentioning it at all. As the time approached for their evening out, he sat idly in front of the TV, flicking from one channel to the next. Pouring himself a large scotch, he lay back in the chair, remembering Mandy as she looked that morning, and letting his mind take things much further than she had allowed.

Catherine appeared at the door, changed from her 'market' clothes into something more suitable for a restaurant. She looked different. He said so.

"Thank you for noticing," she smiled, delighted. "I had my hair done."

"You still smell like a chip shop," he said flatly, as he swept the keys from the table and walked to the car.

The evening was not a success. Bee and Roger arrived late. It always was a matter of surprise to

Catherine that a woman who wore so little should take so long to get dressed. She supposed it must be the make-up. Heavy, lurid, immaculate, Bee drew attention to herself throughout the evening. Roger, whose attention she craved, was distant, vague. Eventually she took her pique in another direction. She made reference to Catherine's 'Big Day Out.' She picked up the theme of loyalty which Catherine had used in her own defence: loyalty to old friends, keeping commitments, letting people down. All these figured heavily in her witty tirade. Bee's heavily outlined eyes flirted expressively at Graham. He smiled but failed to respond. Her remarks, intended to raise a laugh at Catherine's expense, fell into a void. She fell silent for a while. Roger and Catherine chatted.

Roger had always felt some affinity with Catherine. He pitied her, despised her almost. Yet he could see his own weakness reflected in hers. Catherine's response to Graham's years of manipulation and bullying was one of self-sacrifice and loyalty; yet Roger's response to Bee had been a resigned apathy, which lately had soured into a hardening resentment. How he longed to be free of this manipulative and self-obsessed relationship. How trapped he was by his own fear. He asked Catherine about her new venture as he called it.

"I would imagine you're very good at it," he said. "You have a gift for making people feel at ease."

"Thank you," she said. "Actually, Roger, I really enjoyed myself, talking to all the customers, especially the dealers. They're such characters."

Roger laughed. "I bet they've got a few tales to tell. How did you like being one of the workers again?"

"I loved it, although it didn't feel like work. Floss and I were a good team. We laughed a lot today. Haven't enjoyed myself so much in ages!"

Bee broke off her flirtation with Graham, tuned sharply on the pair of them. "Thanks for that, Cath," she said in a mock-offended tone.

Catherine was so tired of the constant innuendo, drip, drip, dripping away.

"I'm sorry, Bee." She sighed. "That didn't come out right. It was just something a bit different, I suppose, that's all."

Bee glanced at Graham before inflicting the hoped-for coup de grace. "And what next, Catherine?" She maintained the jocular note in her voice, "You intend to carry on catering, I suppose."

"I do."

Bee raised her hands in mock despair. "Despite the feelings of your latch-key husband, and your abandoned former best friend, you are determined to pursue your career?" She folded her arms arched her eyebrows, and said to the world in general, "There's loyalty!"

"Don't say any more, Bee," Catherine sighed wearily. "Enough's enough."

"Ooh!" Bee squealed. "Someone's feeling guilty!"

Roger grabbed Bee's arm. "That's enough!" he whispered.

She pulled away. "Get off me!" she hissed. "If Catherine's feeling guilty, that's her problem. I didn't prance off with some stranger knowing my friend needed me."

Catherine's eyes filled with tears. She didn't want a scene. Graham laughed and raised his glass. "Touché!" he snarled.

Catherine stood up. She said, her voice tight with tears, "And neither did I, Bee. Floss is a good friend. I made a promise and I kept it. There is no law that says I must be available to drive you wherever and whenever you wish to go. Don't lecture me on loyalty. I'm only called on by you when your stuck-up Golf club friends aren't around, or when you're too mean to take a taxi."

Bee was, for once quite speechless. Catherine sat down again, startled by her own words. Tears of anger were trying hard to squeeze out from her tight shut eyes. Graham, astonished, was silent for a moment. It seemed like hours. She waited for the irate outburst. She turned as she felt his hand on her shoulder. The look of fury on her face made him bite back his words. She looked strong, impenetrable, magnificent. He collected himself, reclaimed his authority. "Let's go home," he barked. "You drive."

Obediently, she followed him from the restaurant. Catherine slipped behind the wheel, all her sudden bravado gone with the habit of subordination. Driving home, her heart battered against her rib cage as the scene in the restaurant replayed itself. She was alternately embarrassed and indignant. She felt weak, she had given in to her anger, embarrassed herself, humiliated Bee. She would apologise tomorrow. Graham would probably insist on it anyway. They arrived home. Graham strode through the door, pushing her aside. As she walked in, he grabbed her. His breath was thick with whisky. He cupped her face. "You're sexy when you're angry," he leered, pushing himself against her. His lips were wet, almost drooling as he bent to kiss her.

Catherine ducked out of his grip, saying simply, "No." He fell, half-slumped, against the wall, laughing.

"Twice in one day," he hissed, so that she would hear him. "Must be losing my touch."

He shambled up the stairs, fell into bed half-dressed. Catherine sat at the kitchen table, trembling. Graham was so drunk; perhaps he would forget what had happened. She should be feeling triumphant. She had spoken her mind, put him in his place, yet he had only reminded her of his unfaithfulness. She looked across at the telephone. There was a message. She pressed the button, it was Helen.

"Hi, Dad and Mum. I've got some free time this weekend, thought I'd pop down and see you both. I'll be there some time in the afternoon, going back on Monday. See you tomorrow."

No, "Would it be alright?" or, "Do you mind if?" It was convenient for Helen, it must be for her parents. A phone call from their daughter was rare, and visits normally confined to Christmas. Still, Catherine was too tired to wonder why. She made herself a cup of tea and curled up on the armchair in the lounge. Thoughts raced through her head. Thoughts too awful to recognise. All those quiet fears she had suppressed for years were becoming too real to ignore. She fell asleep, marooned in a sea of anxiety.

Nine

Laura and her parents were seated on a bench in their local park. Watching as Simon and Nicky played a two-man rugby game, Nicky scoring a suspiciously high number of tries and Simon appeared to come of the worst in every tackle.

"Well?" She let out a breath as if she had been holding it forever. "Mum? Dad? What do you think?"

Her mother and father looked at her sternly, then at each other. Laura's heart dropped to her stomach. Then, putting his arms around both her and her mother, Laura's father spoke.

"He'll do." He chuckled.

*****

The afternoon went smoothly, Catherine steering the conversation skilfully past any difficult subjects. The talk was mainly about Helen, as usual. She was so like her father. Even Graham's return home did not rock the boat. He was only too pleased to talk of her success, reflecting, as he thought, so well his own.

"Anyway, where have you been Dad? I thought you'd be here to meet me, at least!"

It was as if Catherine did not actually count. Catherine looked over this slight, determined not to spoil this fantasy family time before the inevitable truth was revealed. Why had Helen come home? She was obviously happy, thriving even. In fact, the way she dressed, the way she carried herself, spoke success. There was something more, a beauty about her. Catherine saw it, recognised it, but could not name it.

She watched as the two of them preened and paraded their egos. Graham gave no reason for his absence, only occasionally glancing contemptuously at Catherine. He continued to chat with Helen as if her mother was somewhere else. They began to joke about Simon or "Holy Joe" as they always called him. Catherine tidied away the lunch plates still scattered across the table. As she washed them in the sink, Graham shouted across.

"Dishwasher's down there on the left, you know!"

Helen giggled conspiratorially. Catherine looked out of the window; they could carry on for hours, she knew. She sighed. Just then, there was a sharp knock on the kitchen door, which opened as it was knocked. It was Bee. She rushed across to Helen.

"Darling, you're home, How nice!" She kissed Helen on both cheeks. "It's been an age since we saw you. I've had a brilliant idea. You can't say no, as I've already booked it." She touched Graham's shoulder. "You know me - Miss Impulsive!"

Catherine did not like to point out that Bee was long away from a 'Miss', and could hardly be called impulsive.

"I've booked a restaurant, somewhere special," Bee emphasised, all eyes at Graham. "Our treat. Come round at 7:30. We'll all go in our car. It'll be fun!" She was gone in an instant, leaving silence behind her.

Graham spoke first. "Well, at least someone's making a fuss over you, love."

Even Helen saw the pain this caused her mother. "Don't be mean, Daddy," She teased. "Mum's gone to a lot of trouble to make my room pretty, and at short notice." She pecked Catherine on the cheek and turned to leave the room. "I'm going to have a shower and a lie down; the journey was exhausting. Can you give me a shout at six, Mum? Then I'll start getting ready."

Catherine's belief that Helen had become a carbon copy of her father was not altogether fair. Growing up inside the sham marriage between a self-absorbed bully and his apparently complicit victim had given Helen a horror of counterfeit of any sort. She knew what she wanted, she was clear about it, she worked for it. She trusted no-one, took nothing at face value and was always looking for the self-interest behind any offer of friendship. Helen had shied away from relationships until this clumsy, guileless, beautiful but very 'taken' man had crashed into her life. She fell asleep, trying to plan her way through a very unplanned predicament.

Graham had left the room on the heels of his daughter, muttering something about a phone call.

It was easier this way. Catherine tried hard to pull her thoughts together. He was having an affair, another affair, in fact, after so many promises and lies. This time she must decide. She could see herself reflected in the window as she stood there looking into nothing. She was transparent, invisible unless you looked really hard. Strangely, she felt no sorrow this time, no self-recrimination. She felt tired, so tired.

*****

Bee had already begun to prepare for the evening, it was important that she look as young and alluring as possible, especially with young Helen there to be compared to. Only this afternoon she had bought a sexy white leather bomber jacket, and matching mini-dress. It would be perfect for tonight. She was worried about Roger. He seemed tense, jumpy. She had suggested they all take a taxi, but he insisted that he would drive. Bee decided that a night out was just what he needed to cheer him up. The matter was decided, the restaurant booked.

The Chandlers arrived punctually. Helen was looking radiant and very much her age. Bee having tried and failed to look Helen's age, tried to make it up by being extra vivacious and girlish. They all squeezed into Roger's car. Bee prattled on squeakily about nothing in particular. "You'd better go in the middle, Catherine, balance out the weight! Only joking. Us littl'uns can squash in either side." She sat beside her friend. "It's a mystery tour tonight everyone. My choice. I decided it was high time we tried somewhere new. Drive on, then, Roger." She touched Helen on the knee, who imperceptibly recoiled. "I don't think Roger would get up in the morning if I didn't tell him when! Men, eh?" Catherine and her daughter smiled weakly. "Oh! Honestly, Catherine, those shoes!"

Catherine looked down at her low-heeled brogues.

"You could have dressed up a bit. You look like you're off to do the garden!" This was meant for all to enjoy. Graham sniggered, mumbling something.

Catherine looked embarrassed. "I thought it was something like the usual place. If you'd said, I would have worn something dressier."

"Oh, I daresay there'll be lots of horsy types there, dressed just as scruffily as you are. You'll probably blend right in!"

"Are you sure? I wish you'd said Bee."

Help came, unexpectedly, from Helen. "You look great, Mum, don't worry. We're not going to the hunt ball, are we Bee?"

Bee giggled. "Hardly."

"Or a night-club?" She cast a disparaging eye up and down Bee's tightly fitting dress. Bee glanced down at herself, too.

"No, not a night club. Definitely not a night-club."

She sounded less sure of herself now. This turn of events was disconcerting. Helen and her father could always usually be relied upon to join in with her. For some reason, they were not. Bee changed the subject.

"You'll love this place!" she enthused. "Fantastic food, very classy, historic building. For all you history buffs, it used to be a country house." She looked at Catherine with a strange quality in her gaze.

As they approached this surprise venue of Bee's, Catherine was pleased to see that it really was a beautiful place, a gothic pile, once home to some wealthy Victorian magnate, now a money spinner for some American hotel conglomerate. As they arrived, an obsequious attendant took their coats and showed them to their table.

"This is a charming place, Bee." Catherine smiled as she took in the immaculate table silver, fresh flowers and rich, sumptuous décor. Everything sparkled and shone. "How did you find it?"

Bee smiled a conspiratorial smile. For a moment, her eyes flicked across at Graham then back to Catherine. "Oh, I came here a few years ago. Wondered if the place was still as good now as it was then. I think it's actually improved with age. What do you think Graham?"

"I wouldn't know about that, Bee, since this is my first visit. I do think it's a very impressive hotel though. Let's hope the food lives up to its image."

"Oh, I'm sure it will be every bit as good as it promises to be."

Bee became aware that her flirting and insinuations were rather more obvious than she had intended. Graham looked nothing if not embarrassed. As they took their seats, she turned her attention to Helen.

"You look very striking tonight, Helen," she piped. "That's a very unusual outfit, is it foreign?"

Helen looked up from her menu. "It comes from India," she answered.

"Really! Roger went to India last year." She added, "On business of course." She raised her voice to impress the surrounding diners. "Roger often goes overseas on business trips. At his level it's expected"

"Nothing so glamorous for me," Helen replied rather hastily. "This comes from a shop in London."

"That's a long way to go on a shopping trip!" Bee guffawed at her own wit.

"Actually, it was a gift from a friend."

"Well, he must be a very good friend, to buy such an expensive gift."

"Yes, he is a very dear friend. He said he bought it to match my eyes. I hadn't thought about how much it cost him."

"Well, you should always avoid a cheapskate, Helen, believe me!" Bee laughed too loudly. Again.

Helen smiled, looking uncomfortable.

"I do believe this is serious," Bee squawked. "Go on, Helen, when's the happy day?"

Catherine and Graham were startled at Helen's reaction. Helen, normally cool and confident, was obviously flustered.

She whispered, "Please, Bee, he's just a friend."

The waiter arrived to take their order. Catherine watched, as her daughter composed herself in a moment. There was something different about Helen this time. Maybe she was really in love. It was hard to imagine any one being marvellous enough to overcome Helen's determined ambition and self-interest. Perhaps she had learned a little humility at last.

The evening progressed, oiled along only by Bee's continual innuendo and voluble flirting, punctuated here and there by embarrassed laughter from Graham or Helen. Roger was quiet to the point of being sullen. He flung a few polite words of small talk at Catherine, but then seemed to sink into himself. Bee's teasing and admonishments served only to shut him down still further.

Catherine had felt, from the minute they entered the hotel, that the staff were unduly familiar, with Graham in particular. Then, as she raised a forkful of baby carrots in coriander to her lips, she caught the eye of one of the waiters stationed at the far wall. He looked away quickly smirking. The light of realisation began to dawn on her. She became aware suddenly of the nudges and smirks, between the rest of the staff. She recognised Graham's discomfort; he was eating quickly, and could not wait to leave.

"This is the place," she thought. "He brings them here!" For a moment she couldn't breathe. It seemed to her that she had been paralysed in that ridiculous eating pose for ever. Thoughts raced through her mind now, thoughts she did not want to entertain.

"Are you alright, Catherine?" Roger asked softly. She breathed, startled.

"Fine, fine," she replied automatically. "This is delicious!" She coughed.

Bee was straight in. Like a malicious hawk diving for an easy tid-bit. "Slow down, Catherine. Don't stuff it in so fast, you'll choke!"

Catherine looked at Bee. Her friend. This was the place *she* had chosen. Catherine looked at Bee then at Graham. Surely not, she thought. But she remembered the continuous flirting, the mutual understanding they boasted of. The secret jokes. It was too much. Catherine excused herself from the table, hurried to the ladies' restroom in the lobby. She felt sick, and she was too sad for tears. Too angry to shout. She ran the taps and washed her hands, gallons of water and gallons of soap could not wash the pain away - all those years of saying nothing and doing less.

Steam filled the washbasin and misted the mirror. Catherine could barely see herself reflected a couple of feet from where she stood. She leaned in close to where her face should be.

"Who are you, Catherine?" she whispered. Lost and gone…She began to weep; looked down at her white-knuckled hands, gripping so tightly to the edge of the washbasin.

"If I let go, I will fall," she thought, "and where will I land?"

She inhaled deeply, hot water wasting and winding around the sink. She let go with both hands; with one hand she turned off the tap, with the other she tapped at the steam covered mirror. Two dots for eyes and a frown where her smile should be.

"There you are!" she said.

She slipped quietly into the lobby and ordered a taxi. By the time the others got home she was in bed, had packed her bags and hidden them under the stairs. She would leave in the morning.

*****

As Graham drove to work on Monday morning, with only the remotest feeling of regret at Catherine's discovery of his peccadilloes, he anticipated Mandy's reaction to the situation. She would laugh, no doubt, at his wife's unannounced restaurant departure. She would laugh more to hear that Catherine had stormed out only to go home.

"Silly cow!" Graham swore at his wife under his breath. He pushed her out of his mind as he approached his office.

Helen had been up, drinking tea, when he left. Catherine stayed in bed until she heard the door slam on their fond goodbyes, and the car roar away. She dressed quickly and joined Helen at the table. She was all ready to leave. Her leather overnight bag was beside the back door.

"What time is the taxi coming?" Catherine asked, surprised at this apparent haste to leave.

"After you left in such a hurry last night, Roger offered me a lift back. He's going my way, and it beats taking the train."

Catherine was surprised and pleased at this kindness from her neighbour. Helen was looking at her. "Well, Mum?" she demanded. "Why the huff last night, and the big dramatic gesture?"

Catherine sighed. "It's complicated."

"Don't be pathetic, Mother. They were only teasing; I've heard Dad and Bee knocking you far more than that before. You used to take no notice. You've never stormed off before. Honestly, Mum. You should get some HRT or something. It was so embarrassing. If you thought they were having a go at you before you left, you should have heard them afterwards."

Catherine could not tell her daughter. She could not deface the picture she had of the perfect loyal loving father. It would be a betrayal. "I don't want to talk about it."

Helen tutted and rolled her eyes. "Suit yourself!"

Catherine slipped into her Mother role. "Have you had breakfast?"

"Tea will be fine, Mum."

Unexpectedly, Helen clasped Catherine's hand as she reached for her daughter's cup.

"I do love you, Mum," she urged, looking into her mother's eyes. "Whatever happens."

Helen looked like a little girl once more. The little girl who would strut and giggle and bully her way through the playground, then come running to curl up on her mother's lap, overwhelmed by her own self-confidence. Catherine returned the gesture, stroked her daughter's hair.

"What could happen?" she whispered. "You'll always be my special girl."

There was a tap, tap, on the back door. Helen jumped up to answer it, business-like again.

"That'll be Roger. Time to go." She swung her bag onto her shoulder and opened the door.

Catherine heard Roger say, "Ready?" and saw Helen nod in response, call "Goodbye!" and she was gone.

Catherine ran to the front door to wave from the step. Roger opened the car door for Helen, his hand was in the small of her back. It was an over-intimate gesture, Catherine thought. Helen turned swiftly towards her mother.

"Bye, Mum," she called. "I'll phone."

Catherine closed the door behind her. She calmly pulled her suitcases from their hiding place and loaded them into her car. She drove to Floss' house. Everything in her concentrated on not falling apart. She was calm, she was cool, she told herself. She had made a decision. Now she must stick to it. The new, independent, icy Catherine maintained her new image long enough for the door to open on her friend's smiling face.

"Catherine! What a welcome surprise! Come in!" Catherine began to sob, huge racking sobs, heaving up from the depths of her broken heart.

"Whatever is wrong? Come inside, come on, come on." Floss guided Catherine to the sofa, gave her tissues, tea, asked no questions. Eventually the storm stilled.

"I've left Graham," she announced, in a dead voice. The flat statement was eventually followed by a tearful account of the lie she had been living for so long. No excuses, no self-pity was offered, only liability. She took the blame, but this time she was angry, finished with the charade. The only way out was to leave him to it.

Floss listened, amazed at her friend's capacity to forgive, to continue to give love and loyalty where none was offered in return. As Catherine finished her story, exhausted, she looked for Floss' reaction, half-expecting disapproval. None came. Floss was thoughtful.

"More tea?" Floss said. "Come and help me make it. We need a biscuit. I can't make a decision without chocolate!"

Catherine smiled tearfully. "I must look a mess." She smoothed down her shirt, ran her hand over her hair.

"I'm sorry to dump all this on you, Floss. I started to drive and ended up here."

"Thank God you did!" Floss said, dropping three teabags into the pot. You need a plan of action my dear and running away is definitely out!"

"It is?" Catherine asked incredulously. She had planned it so well, this final escape, and it had taken every ounce of courage that she had to actually go through with it. The shock of what she had done was beginning to creep into her thoughts and weaken her resolve.

They sat at the tiny kitchen table. Floss reached across the table and enclosed Catherine's clasped hands in her own.

"Didn't you once tell me that the house was left to your son?"

"My father left it to him on condition that I live in it as long as I wish."

"Then why give it to Graham?"

Catherine's eyes lit up as she realised the implications of her father's will.

"But I can't throw Graham out!"

"No need to do that, dear." Floss smiled. "No need to change anything at all, on the outside."

"But things have changed so much. I can't carry on as if nothing's happened."

"Oh, but I think you can, Catherine. Things haven't changed at all really. From what you tell me, this state of affairs has been going on for years. You just didn't do anything about it."

Catherine blushed began to cry again. "I know. I've been a fool."

"Now, now. None of that, girl. You've been amazing. Wasted on that idiot, but amazing nonetheless. What I meant was that there has been one very big change, but Graham doesn't know about it yet."

*****

The day moved on. By lunch time, Catherine had begun to develop a calm assurance, she saw things so differently when looking through her own eyes at last, freed from the fear, the lies and the fakery that Graham had held over her for so long. Early afternoon saw a new, improved Catherine pulling into the recycle bay at the multi-storey car park. One by one, she unloaded her bulging suitcases, and heaved each one into the huge Salvation Army donations bin.

"Goodbye, Old Catherine," she smiled, dashing her hands together as if to wipe away her old self.

Then, armed with the credit cards she never used, but which Graham insisted she have, she 'hit the shops,' as Bee called it. Bee would have been proud of her. Stunned, but proud. In only two hours, Catherine filled the equivalent of three suitcases with bright, pretty clothes. "No black, brown or navy, she told the shop assistants.

She changed into a dress of deep red, with a pair of boots that would give Bee's clicky heels a run for their money and hurled the last Old Catherine outfit in the nearest bin. Then the New Catherine drove home.

Bee, of course, was waiting. She pounced as Catherine dragged her many parcels from the boot. "Catherine, you've been shopping?"

"I have." Catherine answered firmly. Bee, undeterred by Catherine's confident tone, began to batter her in the usual way. Throwing words at her hoping to hurt, hoping to hit. "Selfish... Thoughtless... Unfair... Did anything fit?"

Catherine appeared not to notice, which infuriated Bee even more. Instead she just brushed her aside, marching into her home and shutting the door, leaving Bee stranded and confused on her gravel drive. Once inside, Catherine hugged her secret to herself, and tee-hee'd like some cartoon villain.

Ten

Alone in the house, Catherine stripped the beds as usual, and tidied Helen's room. She noticed that the old photograph albums had been pulled from their usual shelf. Helen nostalgic? It seemed unlikely. But then lots of unlikely things were happening lately. As she pegged out the washing, she heard the telephone ring. Must be Graham to say he was on his way. She hurried in, realising that she had not even thought about what to cook, let alone start to make it. As she picked up the receiver, she heard a giggle, then a cough, as the woman on the end of the line regained her composure. There was a smirk in her voice as she spoke.

"Mrs Chandler?"

"Speaking."

"I have Mr Chandler for you."

Graham spoke; it was a conspiracy. "Catherine, I'm all tied up here, I'm afraid, just cannot get away, I'll be really late."

Catherine took a deep breath, time to face it.

"Graham, I know what's going on."

"It's not what you think, Kate. I've really got my hands full." His voice was tight with suppressed laughter.

She could imagine what filled his hands. She remembered all those other times like this one He had always come back to her, and she was now overwhelmed by the enormity of the decision she had made. Without Graham, she would have nothing; there had always been Graham; what would the children think; how would she cope? Why hurt everyone so much over *this* betrayal, when she had let so many others pass?

Suddenly, Old Catherine was back, pleading, fearful.

"Come home, Graham. You work too hard. Come home. I'll wait up for you."

"No, perhaps you'd better go to bed. I could be at this all night."

Catherine could hear the other woman laugh softly, seductively. She must be listening.

"Why don't you do the extra work tomorrow," she pleaded. "I'll make you a nice supper. There's a good film on TV tonight."

Graham yawned his disdain. Pipe and slippers versus forbidden delights. No contest.

"Graham, please. I know what's happening."

"You're pathetic, Catherine. Get a life!" He slammed down the phone and turned his full attention to Mandy. She passed him a brimming champagne glass.

"Here's to us," he said. She smiled cynically. "What us?" She dipped her finger in her glass, ran it down his chest. "You are a married man."

Catherine decided to take a shower. She was angry with herself, her weakness. But she had at least given him a chance. If he had shown one iota of remorse, one speck of concern, she would have allowed things to go on as they had before. At least now she knew for certain that he had no love for her, and no longer the respect to cover up what he was doing. Their marriage was well and truly over. The only question now, was when to cut the tie completely. She was glad her friend had persuaded her not to run away.

"Bide your time," Floss had said, "don't act in haste."

She needed to wait to really decide what she wanted to do. She was growing stronger by the hour. Instead of crumbling, admitting the truth had renewed her. Things looked different. She flicked on the radio, laughing out loud at the coincidence. Someone was belting out 'I Will Survive!'

"Cue the music!" she shouted aggressively, stepping into the shower and joined in with gusto. As she emerged from the shower, Catherine looked in the mirror; steam lacquered the surface, obscuring her reflection. How foolish and accepting she must appear to them both. For a moment the familiar feeling of helpless resignation washed over her.

"No, you don't! No, you don't!" she told her reflection, firmly. "Enough is enough." She reached out and wiped the mirror clean.

"There you are!" she said to the pink and plump figure she saw.

"We'll get a life, shall we? Since Graham is always right about everything, he must be right about this too!"

She grimaced. "But what am I going to do?"

He was right, of course, she must get a life. But now, now, that life no longer relied on Graham for its value or its direction; everything else was uncharted territory. Floss had offered her work every Saturday if she wanted it. Now that she had decided to stay, she was free to watch and wait until it was time to tell Graham to go.

Simon had been inviting her to visit him for months; she felt free to go now. Graham was not to know just yet. She would resume normal service when he eventually returned home. She decided to take up Simon's offer; a short holiday would be an opportunity to clear her thoughts and to meet this girlfriend he was always talking about. She began to imagine herself as mother of the groom, had just picked out her shoes and bag, when the ring of the telephone jolted her back to reality. She grabbed her robe from the door and ran to the bedroom to answer it.

"How are you doing?" It was Floss.

Catherine assured her friend that she was fine, surprisingly so. She recounted her conversation with

Graham; both laughed at Grahams 'advice.' Floss approved heartily of Catherine's plan to visit Simon.

"Ring him as soon as you put the phone down," she said, or you'll change your mind.

"I don't think I will," Catherine remarked, a little put out.

"You can't say how you'll feel once *he* gets home," Floss retorted. "You've got to be decisive my dear, make yourself a woman of action. But not too obviously, though, hey?" They laughed.

*****

Simon wanted to tell his parents about Laura, but he considered their reaction. Mum would be pleased, he hoped. But his father! He knew what Graham would say about Laura and Nicky; he just did not want to expose her to such spite. Perhaps he would just appear with them, deed done. But that would not be fair on Laura. He hardly spoke to his father now, and his mother was squeezed so hard under his thumb she had become almost voiceless and invisible. The trouble was, Laura wanted to marry with the blessing of both parents.

"Time for a pray, I think," he said, looking up. "*You'll* have to sort this one out."

As often happened, before Simon had time to set his problem before his Maker, the answer arrived in a most unexpected fashion. As soon as her conversation with Floss had ended, Catherine made the promised call. She was surprised when a woman answered his work mobile.

"Oh, I'm sorry. I must have the wrong number. I wanted Simon Chandler," she faltered.

"No, you're okay," replied the girl. "This is Simon's number. I'm Laura. I'll get him."

"Hello, Simon Chandler speaking."

"It's Mum," Catherine whispered. "Have I called at an awkward time? Only I thought you didn't...well...you always said you wouldn't... I'm sorry if I interrupted anything."

"Mum, it's alright. Haven't had a sudden lapse into the ways of the world, if that's what you mean. I have been baby-sitting. Laura's been on an evening course."

Catherine blushed audibly. "I only wondered..."

"It's really alright, Mum. Don't worry. It's nice to hear from you. How are you? You sound tired."

Catherine seized the opportunity. "I am tired. Actually, that's why I called. I wondered if the offer to come and stay would be still open?" The tone of Simon's voice was confirmation enough, if any were needed, that he would be delighted to see her.

"Mum, that would be great. When can you come? I thought Dad would never get the time off."

"It would be just me," she said. "I need a break. Without your Dad."

Simon thought he understood; he didn't have enough to offer his father, not enough to make him want to give up a few days at work.

"I understand. When can you come?"

"How soon do you want me?"

"As soon as that, eh?" he said, looking across in coded surprise at Laura. She made a 'who knows' gesture back. She indicated he should ask her up as soon as possible.

"Come as soon as you like, Mum. I'll get the spare room ready."

"Is tomorrow too soon?"

"Tomorrow will be fine. Let me know when the train arrives, and I'll come and pick you up."

"I think I'll drive, Simon. I'll give you a call when I am setting off. I should arrive sometime in the afternoon."

Simon, surprised at his mother's urgency, and the fact that she was taking the car in spite of her hatred of motorway driving, could only say a cheery goodbye. He turned to Laura in stunned silence, mouth agape in exaggerated shock.

"Well?" Laura asked. "What are you waiting for? You've got the spare room to sort out!"

Ignoring the hint about the spare room, Simon tried to make sense of his mothers' remarkable behaviour. "I'm staggered," he said, "suddenly she wants to visit, on her own. Something's up, something's definitely up!"

*****

"Graham and Mandy," he toasted.

"Mandy and Graham," she returned.

They had spent the afternoon at her place. She had charmed and fascinated him. He was at her mercy. She knew it; she revelled in it.

He felt chosen, which he was; she had chosen him but, whether she knew it or not, her motives for having the affair were not relevant. Today was the day, he had decided, to end the affair. He was getting too attached to Mandy. She was becoming too important, and all he thought about. He would have this night, then break it up; maybe not straight away, but very soon, before things got too serious. How Mandy felt, he could not tell, he only assumed that she was even more attached than he was, because they always were. Graham so loved himself, he could not imagine things any other way.

Mandy, however, was approaching things from another direction entirely. It seemed to her that things were falling in nicely with her plan. That silly wife of his was turning out to be more of a problem than she had anticipated. He had been troubled after the telephone conversation. It was meant to make him laugh, feel daring, adventurous. Instead he sighed.

"She told me," he said, as they lay in bed. "She knows what's going on."

He drew his knees up to his chin, wrapped his arms around them, and rested his head on them. He was all closed off. She thought for a moment, then put her hand on his arm, but he withdrew it as if she had burned him. Strange, he had never shown any conscience at all before now. He had made such a point of his wife's disinterest and her stupidity. He sighed heavily again. She realised this was the time to act if she meant to hold on to him. He expected her to cajole him, cling to him. Instead she slid from the bed began to dress. Surprised, he looked up from his despondent state, watching. She was not so much dressing as doing a reverse striptease. With slow, sinuous movements she put on a camisole and stockings, then a soft shapeless dress in a rich golden colour, it clung to every soft contour of her body. She bent over, brushing her hair fiercely, then flung her head back, her curls falling into place.

She looked at him, hands on hips. "Well. That's that, then." She pushed her feet into high heeled mules; they emphasised the curve of her legs.

He was confused. Overwhelmed. He had been just about to launch into his, "It's been great, but..." speech. She was supposed to cry, beg, plead. Then, one last night together before poor dutiful Graham returned to his neurotic demanding wife. Instead, Mandy was unmoved. Her mood could almost be described as

165

indifferent, it seemed. She stopped at the doorway, looked back. "Coffee or tea?"

He was dazed. "What?"

"I thought you'd like a cup of something before you go, unless you have to dash off straight away."

His look was vacant, empty, uncomprehending. Mandy saw her strategy was working. She wanted to laugh; his expression resembled a baby whose toy had been snatched away. She hurried off to make coffee, a smile of triumph playing on her lips.

"You'd better get dressed!" she shouted back over her shoulder. He crawled from the bed, sat on the edge, his eyes tracing the patterns on the Oriental rug. All the time she had been agreeing with him that this was a no strings, no commitment thing, and she really meant it. He found it hard to believe she was not at all in love with him. They always fell in love with him, always. And Catherine on the phone, with her half-hearted attempts to get him back; he felt adrift. Something unfamiliar was creeping through his mind, a creature unrecognised, but not unknown. He could almost name it, almost see it.

She returned with two cups of very aromatic coffee on a tray. It did not occur to him that the usual place for a farewell coffee would be the sitting room, or even the kitchen. It did not occur to him that he was playing into her hands. She put the tray on the dressing table, in the window which was a few feet from the end of the bed. Then walking back to him, she said, briskly,

"Not dressed yet? Come on lazy bones!" She didn't sit, but stood beside him, towering over him in her high heels. He looked up, helpless. He finally identified that feeling. He was afraid.

"I don't want to go." He hoped his voice did not sound as weak and pleading as it sounded to him. She appeared not to notice, inside she relished every moment of his agony.

"I don't think you mean that, Graham. When you spoke to your wife, you changed. I thought everything was over between you two, that you had some sort of understanding."

"You made me phone!" he retorted, like a petulant child. He glowered.

Mandy turned away, he was pathetic. So easy to make him dance to her tune, this arrogant, self-assured, and now bewildered man. She picked up her cup and began to sip at the coffee. Her eyes met his, he looked away. His mind was racing, how did he get here? He knew where he stood with Catherine; biddable, predictable, boring. Why, now of all times, had she decided to make a fuss? He looked up at Mandy. Beautiful, bewitching Mandy. She seemed to be waiting for something. He felt vulnerable, sitting naked on the bed, covered only by a sheet. His clothes were on a chair across the room. His confidence even faltered at the thought of walking to the chair and having to dress himself while she, composed and covered, looked on.

Indecision paralysed him. It was a strange, frightening feeling.

Swiftly, she cracked her empty cup down onto the dressing table, strode towards him and whipped the sheet away. Instinctively he covered himself with his hands.

"Get dressed," she barked. "Then come into the sitting room."

He did not see the smile Mandy wore as she left. As he entered the sitting room, she bore the patient expression of a cat stalking a mouse. Leafing through some stylish magazine, she did not look up as she directed him to sit. He waited expectantly. He had even made the bed, carried the coffee cups into the kitchen, things he would never do at home. When he and Catherine had first been married, he had made some attempts to please, but that had all stopped years ago. Since then he had really only pleased himself. Now Mandy was there. He so wanted to please himself with her, but she wasn't playing the game. He was under her spell. He felt hypnotised, gradually regressing into childhood, aware of the responses he was making, but unable or unwilling to control them. The few moments it took for her to close the magazine and lay it carefully aside seemed like years. Years that were snatched away from him as he waited. He tried to read her expression. It occurred to him that the signs of anxious expectation that should be on her face now, were actually on his. She spoke.

"Graham."

"Yes." he blurted. He realised he had been holding his breath. She must be able to see his agitation. To make matters worse, he could not stop himself from taking in a huge gulp of air to replace the one he had just let out. It was a great gasping slurp of air. He sounded as if he were about to burst into tears. He was an awkward youth again, eager to please, trying to project a self-assurance he did not feel.

She was in the armchair, he on the sofa, the coffee table between them. She was barricaded in. He was isolated, getting younger every minute. She looked into his eyes and leaned forward. "Where do we go from here?"

His eyes flicked to the television. It was nine o'clock. Time for the news, he thought, immediately aware of the irrelevance of this thought. His gaze returned to Mandy. She was silent, eyebrows raised, waiting for an answer he couldn't give. He tried to laugh it off, but his laugh became an embarrassed giggle as it left his mouth.

"I don't know what you mean, er, what do you want? I mean, I don't quite...sort of..."

The tongue-tied teenager he had become could not look at her. His voice trailed away as his eyes turned and rested again on the television.

"Graham!" she shouted. He jumped. "Will you look at me when I'm talking to you!"

He realised he had been looking at the TV screen.

"Are you thinking of going home and watching that film with your wife?"

He shook his head sullenly. "No, I just can't think straight when I look at you. You're so lovely, Mandy. I...well...I just want to be with you."

"I want to be with you, too, Graham. That's the problem."

He was totally confused now. They both wanted the same thing; how could that be a problem? His question must be written on his face. She answered it.

"We both know you have done this sort of thing before, Graham, don't we?"

He nodded, feeling strangely close to tears. There, alone on his side of the room, he waited for her to explain things to him, to reassure him.

"Has your wife ever made a fuss about your little flings before?"

"No, she hasn't, just pretended not to know."

She went to speak, but he cut across her, eager to make his point. "But this isn't just a fling, Mandy," he whined.

She put her hand up to stop him speaking and flashed him a smile of warm approval. "Exactly," she said.

As if he had won a competition, he felt rewarded.

"Exactly. Maybe she is afraid that things are different this time. She thinks she's losing you."

"That must be it." Graham was more than satisfied with this explanation. It flattered him to think of a woman fighting to keep him, even if it was only Catherine. He still felt a lot was riding on his answers to Mandy's questions; he sensed she was not finished yet.

She watched him struggling with his thoughts. This was so easy. If she had not convinced herself that she was fond of him, it would be easy to despise him, all puffed up with his own self-importance, and so easily deflated into this demanding, insecure fool. He was ready. It was make or break now, and if things went wrong, she would have to start all over again with someone else.

"Is she right, Graham, do you think?"

He nodded.

"Well, is she losing you?"

He looked at the floor thoughts racing and tumbling through his head, all he could grasp was his overriding desire for this woman.

"Yes, Mandy, she is."

She smiled again, a forgiving smile, wordlessly beckoning him towards her.

Eleven

When Catherine awoke suddenly in the early hours of the morning, it was still dark. She felt the bed beside her, it was empty and cold. She listened for the sound of Graham's key in the door. Perhaps it was his car arriving that woke her up. She waited. Nothing. Creeping to the window, she saw only the empty driveway. The sky was beginning to lighten behind the stars. She wrapped herself in her dressing gown, went downstairs and, like a typical Englishwoman in a crisis, made tea.

Today's the day, she thought, remembering that clichéd old saying from her teens. "Today is the first day of the rest of your life," she intoned solemnly.

She repeated it loudly, then broke into song, putting the words in an instant opera somewhere between 'Eine Kleine Nachtmusik' and the 'Pirates of Penzance.' Carefully, she washed the teapot and mug, wiped the kitchen surfaces and then climbed the stairs and packed. Within half an hour she was ready to go, it was only six thirty.

"Now is not the time to hesitate," she told herself loudly, wondering if talking to herself was good therapy, or merely a sign of incipient mental collapse. Just one call before she left. She telephoned Simon to let him know she was on her way and would be there around lunch time. He told her to come to the church. It was his turn at the Centre, and much easier to find than the flat.

"Mum," he said, "I have something to tell you..."

"Can't you tell me now, love?"

"No, Mum, I want to tell you face-to-face."

Catherine smiled to herself as she said her goodbyes, and on impulse ran upstairs to her jewellery box and removed a small green leather case, slipping it into her handbag. With that, she locked the door and jumped in the car, her small suitcase already stashed away in the boot.

"Let's get going!"

A few hours later, she stopped at what she considered to be about halfway. It was already mid-morning. Newport Pagnell sounded like some sleepy little village tucked away under a craggy hill. Instead, its motorway services were all neon-lit concrete, carpeted by identical sales reps' saloon cars. Catherine sipped at the bitter coffee she had purchased. She should have been stunned by her own daring, but it was as if she was an onlooker to the journey she was taking. She thought how useful the ability to shut off all feeling was. Then she realised that it was her failure to face up to the unpleasantness in her life that had put her here in the first place. That was before, she said to herself. This is now. Now is my future.

She telephoned Floss, who was both thrilled and amazed at this sudden departure. Again, she found herself at the opposite end of a conversation where her every word was repeated.

"You've left already then, Catherine. Well, I must say I'm delighted for you. Shocked, but delighted."

"Don't you approve?"

"Approve? My dear, I approve wholeheartedly. You need a break away from him." She could not bring herself to mention Graham's name, it seemed. "Best thing for you. I just didn't think you would get going so soon! Good for you!"

"I'm coming back on Friday, so I'll be able to help you out on Saturday at the market, if you still want me."

"*Of course* I still want you, but you mustn't hurry back just for that...No dear, you wouldn't be letting anyone down. Just enjoy your time with your son, Simon." She emphasised these last words rather unnecessarily, Catherine thought.

"Floss..."

"Yes dear?"

"Is Andrew there with you?"

"Well yes, as a matter of fact he is...Why?"

"Floss, you are dreadful!"

"I know I am!" They laughed.

"Good luck, Catherine. Now stick to your decision, remember. Don't give in!"

"I won't give in Floss, promise. Bye, Floss. Bye Andrew!"

Now, time to make the most important phone call of the day. She felt strangely excited as she called Graham's office; the secretary answered. There was some confusion as Mr Chandler had not arrived yet.

"In fact, he just called to say he'd be late as his wife is sick and he has to take her to the doctors," the woman informed Catherine. "If you leave your name and number, I will give him a message as soon as he gets in."

"And how soon do you think that will be?" Catherine asked in a business-like tone.

"Oh, I'm sure he'll be in as soon as he can. Mr Chandler is very reliable."

Catherine choked back a laugh. "What is your name, please?"

"Mrs Marchment, his secretary."

"Well, thank you very much for your help, Mrs Marchment, it's been nice to talk to you."

"Oh, thank you. Ah, is there any message?"

Catherine considered her response for a moment. She thought about this being the first day, and so on. "Yes, there is a message," she said. "Do you have a pen and paper?"

The woman assured her she was ready to take any message.

"Tell Mr Chandler his wife called..."

She could almost hear the faithful Mrs Marchment cringe.

"…I am visiting our son Simon for a few days. So, when he does get home, I won't be there. Tell him I'll be back for work at the weekend."

The strangled shock at the other end of the telephone gave Catherine an unexpected thrill.

"Very well, Mrs Chandler."

The voice was suddenly louder. Catherine could hear the buzz of the office and realised that Mrs Marchment was calling their conversation to the attention of the rest of the office.

"I'll pass your message on, that you're visiting your son and will be back at the weekend. Is that it?"

"Yes, thank you very much for your help." She was surprised at the woman's parting shot.

"Not at all, Mrs Chandler." She enthused, "It will be a pleasure to give Mr Chandler that message. Goodbye!"

Catherine smiled to herself as she returned the receiver to its cradle. The woman's voice had been warm and friendly. She had expected hostility. To hear Graham's account of his office life, you would think he was Mr Popularity. It began to dawn on her that that may not be the case.

*****

Laura was nervous. Simon could tell she was nervous, although she insisted, as she stood on the doorstep at 7:30 that morning, that she was merely being efficient.

"That spare room of yours needs sorting out!" she announced briskly, as she marched past him into the tiny sitting room.

From the two enormous bags she had lugged in, she began to pull various items of cleaning equipment. Then, unbelievably to Simon, she produced freshly ironed sheets, some sort of artificial flower arrangement and a large glass vase. Incredibly, the bags were still bulging. Suddenly Laura stopped her excavations and stood straight, one hand on her forehead.

"I've forgotten something," she said, raking her mind for the elusive something, whatever it was.

Simon, who had stood statue-like and bewildered as this strange scene played out before him, realised at last that he was not dreaming.

"Laura, I've got polish and a duster. What's wrong with..."

She waved him to silence with a flapping motion of her free hand...then turned to look at him in horrified realisation. "Nicky!" she yelled.

Simon, wide eyed with shock, replied, "You've not left him at home?"

Laura rushed out of the door and ran down the stairs. "Don't be daft, he's in the car!"

Simon, still half asleep, decided some action was called for. He went and got dressed. As he emerged from the bedroom, Nicky flew through the open front door.

"Simon!" he squealed, throwing himself at him. Minutes later, the two of them were eating breakfast, as Laura continued with her inexplicable assault on the spare room.

"What's got into your mummy?" Simon whispered.

Nicky leaned forward, confidentially. "I don't know. We've cleaned our place all up and now we've got to do yours too."

"But why have you got to do so much cleaning?"

The boy looked at Simon as if he were a moron. "Because your mummy's coming to see us, and we don't want her to think we're dirty, useless people, do we now?"

Simon wanted to laugh at this tiny replica of Laura, so obviously repeating his mother's words.

"But you two are perfectly fine as you are!" Simon protested.

Nicky sighed, world weary. "I know, Simon," he said. "I told her that already, but she won't listen, just keeps washing and scrubbing and ironing and everything, like mad!"

At that moment, Laura appeared at the door. "I don't know what the lad's been saying," she said, firmly, "but I'm just trying to make sure your mother feels welcome. That's all."

Simon remained perplexed. "There's really no need for all this fuss, Laura my love. I'm sure she'll be happy just to be here."

Laura was upset. "Well that's all you know, Simon Chandler. I suppose you'd be happy for your poor mother to sleep in that damp grotty room, under that horrible, dusty duvet surrounded by old postcards and car magazines!"

If he was honest, Simon would have to admit that this was exactly the case. Wisely, however, he did not say so. Laura was in full flow again.

"I just brought a few things round to brighten the place up, that's all. You'll see what I mean when I've finished."

"How do you know my mum doesn't like dust and old car magazines anyway?" Simon asked, trying to lighten the mood a bit. He failed. Laura looked at him with pitying resignation.

Nicky took a deep breath, "And she doesn't like hairy people, either, Simon."

They both looked at Nicky and he looked at his mother. "She doesn't mummy, does she?" To clarify the point, Nicky folded his arms triumphantly and explained to Simon. "Mummy has already shaved her legs and her arms and plucked her eyebrows before she came here!"

By the time Catherine telephoned, the little flat was spotless. Simon had to admit that, although he always kept the place in good order, Laura's touch had made it shine. The spare room, crisp and colourful in its new linen, had a pale floral rug. The bathroom was sparkling and smelling of lemons. The kitchen had crystal clear windows and a pot plant on the sill. Every room was essentially the same, but somehow different. Better different. As they left for the drop-in centre, he slipped his arm around her waist, kissed her gently. "Thank you, Laura," he whispered. "The place looks amazing!"

Nicky grabbed his free hand. "I did the polish," he trilled. Simon planted a kiss on the top of his head. "You're amazing too" he said.

*****

Helen looked at her reflection in the tiny mirror above the sink. The staff would be arriving soon. She felt dreadful, looked worse. She slapped on some make up, too much blusher. "I look like Bee," she thought. Then she wiped it off with both hands. Sighing heavily, Helen turned to unlock the back door, steadied herself as another wave of nausea hit her. One of the stylists pushed through the door making her stumble backwards.

"Oh, sorry, Helen, didn't see you. Are you all right? You look dreadful."

So much for the make-up. Helen mumbled something about food poisoning and disappeared into the toilet again. She emerged a few minutes later to find the rest of the staff had arrived and were getting about their business. Helen tried several times to go into the salon itself, but the chemical stink and the heat just made her sick. She excused herself and left.

*****

Three days with Simon and his 'instant family' were enough to show Catherine that her son had found his true love. She and Laura were friends from the outset. She found this determined young woman to be at once vulnerable and courageous. Catherine helped out at the St Christopher's House centre, talking to the regulars as if she had known them forever. It was after the lunch time rush, as they were drying dishes that Laura spoke.

"You don't have to do all this work you know, Mrs Chandler. Really, it's very kind of you."

"Oh, Laura, call me Catherine, please, and I love helping out here. Everyone is so friendly."

"Um…" Laura twisted her tea towel backwards and forwards between her hands. "How do you feel about me and Simon?"

"If you mean, 'can I see you two growing old together?' the answer is yes. And if you mean 'do I approve?' then the answer is also yes. Of course, I do

Laura, I am so happy Simon has found someone he can be happy with. Really, I know how important it is."

Laura took another breath. "I am not sure if you know my background... Nicky is..."

"Nicky is a darling child and a credit to you. That's all there is to it, Laura. Honestly, Simon told me your story, and, if anything, it makes me admire and respect you even more."

Laura looked up at her. Catherine held out her arms. "Come here, daughter-in-law," she said. And they hugged.

*****

Helen looked at her body in the mirror. Her fitted suit had been uncomfortably tight. There was a deep red line where the waistband had cut into her flesh. Who knew that things would start to change so soon? She put on track suit pants and a vest, left the changing room and stepped on the treadmill. As arranged, he walked in ten minutes later and joined her in the line of runners. They jogged along in companionable silence for some time, but Helen had to stop before the usual half hour was up.

"What's wrong?" he asked, "can't take the pace?"

She smiled and made her way to the swimming pool, did her lengths and then returned to the changing room. He joined her in the restaurant soon afterwards. She drank mineral water. These snatched moments were treasured by them both and used up greedily as if there would be no more meetings.

*****

Friday morning, and Catherine, Simon, and Laura were walking back from dropping Nicky at school. The conversation turned to Graham and Catherine knew she had to come clean. She told them as gently as she could that her marriage was in some difficulty. Expecting shock or sorrow, Catherine was stunned by Simon's reaction. She stopped in her tracks.

"At last!" He shouted, "at last!"

They sat on a bench as Simon revealed to Catherine the full extent of his distrust and even dislike of his father. Years of verbal taunts, impossible standards and hypocrisy… Catherine could hardly sit still as the true understanding of what he was saying began to dawn.

"Do you mean you knew? How long?" she asked.

"Mum, Helen and I have known for years. The strange thing is, instead of just hating *him*, it was you we despised for allowing him to make fools of us all, bullying us all, sleeping with anything with a pulse. Yet we still wanted his attention, his approval. And now at last, you have had enough."

"But I did it for you children…"

"No, Mum. Be honest, you never asked us. As soon as we could, Helen and I left home. Didn't you realise then what you had put up with for so long?"

Catherine wept quietly. "Oh Simon, I thought I was protecting you, but…so much damage has been done, and now …" Catherine realised at that moment what her children had known for years, that the marriage she had been fighting for was no marriage at all. It was clear that her own stubborn refusal to acknowledge her mistake was the only thing that bound her to a man who despised her.

Laura looked at Simon, with a 'give your mum a break look.' She stood and knelt in front of Catherine, taking Catherine's hands in her own. "Look at your two children, Catherine. Helen is a successful businesswoman and Simon is…." she looked lovingly at him and then back at his mother "…well, you know."

Catherine nodded, tearfully. Laura continued "In spite of everything, Catherine, the love you gave your children meant they grew up with the confidence to strive for what they believe in."

"Yes!" Catherine said, squeezing Laura's hand. "I do know. Thank you."

"Now," Laura went on, "you must look after yourself. You might be free at last, but it's all happened very quickly. You need some time for yourself, do something that's just for you." Laura and Catherine stood and hugged, the three of them walked on toward

Simon's home, chatting on the way about Catherine's future and theirs. They reached her car.

"Well, that's my cue," said Catherine, giving them a final hug, she jumped into the car and wound down the window to say goodbye.

Laura had been fumbling in her bag and taking a business card from her purse she pushed it into Catherine's handbag on the passenger seat. "Take a look later," she said, "it's always helped me."

Catherine drove away with undue haste. Just far enough to get around the corner, pull over and have a jolly good cry. She pulled a tissue from her handbag and as she did so, the little business card fell on to the seat. Catherine picked it up. It was not a business card after all, but a verse from the bible.

> *"The Lord is close to the broken-hearted and saves those who are crushed in spirit." Psalm 34:18*

Simon hugged Laura to him as they walked up the stairs to his flat. "Don't be too hard on her Simon," Laura said. He smiled as they walked into the kitchen to pick up his keys to the hall, and there on the table was a small, black leather jewellery box with a note, which read:

Simon,
This engagement ring belonged to my
dear mother, your grandmother and to her
grandmother before that. It is yours now
With all my love,
Mum xx

Inside the case lay an exquisite sapphire and diamond engagement ring. For the second time in a week, Simon knelt and asked Laura to be his lawful wedded wife.

Twelve

Catherine rang her father from the service station as she travelled back. She needed her Dad; she wanted to unburden herself of the years of self-deception, to tell him about her plans and, most of all, the details of Simon's engagement and her charming daughter-in-law to be. She arranged to drop in on her way home.

"Why not pick up some fish and chips, Cathy?" he asked. "It will be like old times."

"Oh, I don't think…" she began, knowing that Graham would be expecting a meal on the table when he got home. "Oh why not?" she said, "I'll be with you at five, warm the plates up!"

John was delighted to hear of the engagement and touched to know that his darling wife's engagement ring had been entrusted to his beloved grandson. They stood at the sink, he washing the plates and she drying them, as they had done for years.

"There's something else, Catherine, isn't there?" he said, putting his soapy hand on her shoulder. "Come on, you can tell your dear old dad, can't you?"

It seemed that all the tears she had swallowed, all the regret she had buried, all the anger she had locked away unexpectedly surged out of her. She pressed the tea towel with both hands against her mouth but not fast enough or hard enough to stop the swell of hurt exploding in loud painful sobs.

"Oh, Dad," she cried, as he enfolded her in a gentle hug "I've been a selfish fool!"

Nearly an hour later, Catherine had recovered her composure. She drove away from that dear, comforting place, knowing that her father loved her, supported her and had hoped for many years that his daughter would escape her bullying, adulterous husband.

As she arrived home, she realised the house was empty. There were some dirty cups in the sink, but otherwise no sign that Graham had been in the house at all. She filled the sink with hot water and began to wash the cups as Graham lumbered through the door and threw himself onto the sofa, switching on the TV.

"Mine's a coffee!" he ordered. She carried their coffees through to lounge, gave him his, and asked what he wanted to eat. He looked up from his phone, "Nothing, I've eaten already."

To his irritation, she smiled back, "Oh, that's good, so have I."

She took her customary chair beside the fire. Graham, predictably did not even ask where she had been for the last few days. So wrapped up was he in his phone and his own fantasy world. A world where he could do as he liked with no regard for anyone but himself. Graham, like a silly teenager with a crush, constantly texted, emitting the occasional chuckle. Catherine herself felt detached. So much so that she didn't share the news of Simon's engagement.

The house phone rang. Graham snatched it up, but soon handed it over to Catherine when he found it was only Simon calling.

"Yes, I got back a while ago," she responded to Simons query, then continued to chat about her delightful few days in the North.

Graham tutted loudly and turned up the volume on the TV programme to which he had paid no attention to until the phone rang. Catherine stood and put her finger to her ear to better hear her son. "Sorry," she called, "I had better go. Give my love to everyone and a big hug to Laura and Nicky."

She walked towards Graham and replaced the phone in its cradle, Graham frowning and exaggeratedly craning his neck to see the TV as she apparently blocked his view. He sighed loudly and turned the TV off all together.

"So that's where you've been then, looking over Simon's latest squeeze. Well, is she some northern lady vicar then, the Vicar of Burnley, eh? Hahahaha!" He choked with laughter at his own wit. Catherine remained silent as she walked to the door.

"Well?" he snapped.

"Actually, Simon and Laura have been seeing each other for over two years. She works for the same charity as Simon, and is studying to be a social worker.

"Oh, give me strength!" he sighed loudly, "another bleeding-heart do-gooder. They'll do well together. All paid for by the great British taxpayer!"

"Well, they just got engaged, if you are interested."

"Oh, great! His holiness is tying the knot. I suppose we will have to go to some hideous church shindig."

Catherine walked to the bottom of the stairs, "Actually, Graham, I don't think you're invited! Goodnight!"

*****

Next morning, Catherine joined Floss at the market as promised. Their talk, snatched between making steaming drinks and sizzling sandwiches, was of new beginnings. Catherine's new beginnings. Catherine recounted her conversation with Laura.

"That young lady has a lot of sense!" declared Floss, approvingly. "She's absolutely right; you must find something that is purely selfish pleasure. I know you can't imagine yourself not waiting on people or cleaning up after them or some other very worthwhile cause."

She was quite right, of course. Catherine's idea had been to volunteer as a hospital visitor or home help, something useful.

Floss said, "No, Catherine. That will not do at all!"

Floss was determined to make Catherine understand. "Tell me something you enjoy, something you always wanted to do, maybe."

Catherine stared back, blankly. Floss sighed, half laughing, half exasperated.

"Think, girl! What about in school? What did you like then?"

Catherine dredged her memory. Far, far down she found a time when there was not Graham. There she was in her room writing an article for the school magazine. In fact, she had written several articles and even a few short stories. But that was years and years ago.

"Well?" Floss jerked her out of her reminiscences.

Catherine smiled. "There is something." She seemed surprised. "I used to write. Of course, I stopped when I married Graham. I did try to join an evening class once, but... well, you can guess."

Her voice tailed away as her mind filled with all her attempts at some life of her own. She never knew, until now, how completely her own personality had been swallowed up by the leviathan of Graham's ambition and ego. Floss could see the ghastly realisation on

Catherine's face. She looked like someone who has arrived at a gala ball dressed as a carnival chicken.

"I think writing would be perfect, you have the heart of a storyteller, Catherine. Now it's your turn." She thought for a moment as they stacked the tables away at the end of the day. "There's a thing called 'The Storytellers Circle' advertised in the library. They meet at the sixth form college. We could go along, if we don't like it, we don't have to go again."

"We?" Catherine asked.

"Of course, we." Floss replied. "I've never had the nerve to go before, it would be better if we both went. What do you say? Shall we give it a go?"

Arrangements were made, enquiries were made, a laptop carefully selected and bought, and the following Wednesday found the two ladies outside the College. Catherine had expected to find a room filled with 'arty' types. However, these were very ordinary people with a common need to express something in words.

At the first few meetings, they were asked to write a poem, and a piece of research, and Catherine wrote competently for both. But her fortunes really turned on the third meeting. Catherine would always remember that meeting as the day that changed her life or rather brought her back to life.

They were asked to write a piece, 'A Day in My Life.' Some of the circle groaned, but as Catherine began to write, she began to laugh. They took their assignments home and were to present them the following week. For the rest of the week, Catherine spent every spare moment tapping at her laptop. Graham, if he was home, would find her staring at him, then writing furiously with the hint of a smile on her lips.

The day of the Circle came, each of them presented their pieces, and everyone received murmurs of polite appreciation. Catherine, however, was rewarded with roars of laughter, and, at the end, a round of applause. The following week, her piece, 'My Finest Hour,' received a similar response. Her tutor and classmates urged her to enter her work into a competition being run by the local newspaper, The Echo. The winner of 'The Echo New Writers Award' would see their winning article and two subsequent pieces published both in the newspaper and online.

"Write what you know, something you would like to read yourself," her tutor had insisted, when Catherine was lost for inspiration and daunted by the thought of being officially in print.

The telephone was ringing as Catherine came through the door. Graham was in the lounge, whisky in hand, but evidently was too engrossed in his TV to pick up the telephone. Catherine ran to grab the phone in the kitchen. It was Simon, they had the opportunity to come down to London for a few days, and were hoping to visit Catherine and Graham, and, of course Simon's beloved Granddad, during the trip. Catherine was thrilled.

"You can stay in your old room," she said, "and Laura and Nicky can stay in Helen's."

"No need Mum, we are going to stay with Granddad."

There was no need to read between the lines. Simon was not going to subject Laura to Graham any longer than he had to. They chatted more and Catherine managed to persuade Simon that they would have a little get together to celebrate the engagement. Catherine hung up the phone.

"That was Simon. They're coming to visit next weekend, staying at Dad's, but I thought we could have a get together here to celebrate the engagement."

Graham grunted his assent and then continued to ignore her.

"You won't forget, will you, next Saturday."

"For God's sake, woman!" he bellowed. "What's your problem? Yes! Next Saturday. Yes! Yes! Okay!"

Catherine, surprised that for once she did not feel fear, guilt or even hurt at her husband's behaviour curled up in her chair, laptop resting on her knees.

She was excited, suddenly inspired with the prospect of writing for the competition. She had remembered the pile of gossip magazines at 'Salon Maurice'. She had turned to the Agony Aunt section in each one. Some 'problems' genuine, and some very obviously contrived to promote the latest gadget or gimmick. She thought of the comedy and tragedy of the life she now led. The words she had never said, the secret, joyful power she had found in writing. Smiling, she tapped her title into the keyboard

"WHAT'S YOUR PROBLEM?"

A fictitious no-nonsense Agony Aunt wrote candid, comic, yet deeply perceptive answers to equally fictitious, but universally recognised dilemmas. Graham had long gone to bed when Catherine completed her 'Problem Page.' For reassurance, and moral support she emailed it to Floss, along with an invitation to the engagement celebration. Floss sent a one line reply next morning

"Hilarious! Send it off and don't change a word!" Catherine did exactly that and, having emailed her entry to the Echo New Writers Competition, waited nervously to hear from them.

Over the next week, Catherine helped her father prepare for his house guests, baked, cooked and deep-froze everything she could in advance. She ordered a cake and invited anyone who she thought might want to join the celebration, along with a few of Simon's old school friends with whom he remained in contact. Of course, Catherine had invited the neighbours, including Bee and Roger, and, for her own pleasure, Floss and Andrew.

*****

They were almost home to Helen's house, she sat with her head leaning on the half-open car window.

"You're not in a train, you know," her lover said, stroking her shoulder. "We can put the air con on."

"Sorry," she said absentmindedly, closing the window, but continuing to stare out of it at nothing in particular.

"Is everything okay?" he asked, glancing across at her, knowing full well that it was not.

"Now that you ask me, I have to be honest and say it's not."

"In what way?"

"In an impossible way, I'm afraid. There's no point in talking about it."

"When we got together, you said no strings… it's just, I never expected to feel so strongly," he said.

Helen looked at him and laughed. No strings…how had she ever got into this? A bit of forbidden fun had turned into a lifetime commitment.

He pulled over into a lay-by near her home. He took her hand. She looked out of the window again. "It's messing with my head."

He touched her hair as she looked towards him and said, "Neither of us expected to feel this way…but the fact is, Mr Secret Lover, your 'other half' will never give you up. I don't want to love you, but I do."

He took her face in his hands. "And I can't spend the rest of my life knowing you are there and knowing we can never be together. You, always so close, but... Oh Helen, I'm so sorry!"

"Sorry? Sorry is no good anymore. I can't have a relationship with sorry. I can't spend the evening with sorry, can I? You're so tied to her... God only knows why. You're still together, and yet you say you love me."

"I do love you! So much." He looked in agony. Helen knew she was being unreasonable. She returned his touch.

"No, love, I am sorry. Sorry for dragging you into this reckless affair. I had my eyes open and now I am behaving like a silly, love-struck girl."

They clung to each other, both aware that this was the end. He spoke first.

"Look, I promise, soon..."

Helen squeezed the tears away from her eyes. She would have to be practical for both of them, try to get back to her old, ice cold self. She took a deep, angry breath. "Oh, just drive me home, will you? I don't want to discuss it anymore! Or ever again!"

As he pulled into her driveway, she wrenched her suitcase and overnight bag from his car and marched into her house, without looking back.

Thirteen

Catherine had fetched her father to her home so he would be there to greet everyone as they arrived. Helen arrived with Roger who had kindly picked her up from Birmingham again. Almost simultaneously, Simon's old car appeared and out tumbled Nicky, Laura and Simon. Catherine greeted them all with enthusiasm as they bundled into the house and sorted themselves out. As small children do, Nicky made a beeline for the oldest person in the room. He introduced himself to John.

"Are you the Granddad?" he asked, without a shred of self-consciousness.

"I am," replied John.

"Where's your dog, then?"

John, amused by the boy's direct manner, pointed through the French windows to the garden where Deefer the dog was banished.

Nicky grabbed John by the hand. "Come on, then," he said, and the two of them marched through the kitchen and into the garden, where Deefer, all wags and barks, awaited.

*****

Graham of course was working late, which meant he was really with Mandy in her smart little flat. They lingered over a light meal. Mandy was the first to speak, which was the usual pattern these days.

"Aren't you supposed to be somewhere tonight, Graham?"

"No." He stretched back in his chair. "That's tomorrow. My reverend son has got engaged and there's a celebration. Half the street is going to be there." Yawn.

Mandy saw an opportunity to find out some more about the size and extent of his divorce settlement. She knew Graham had a large house, and no small children to complicate matters. Everything should divide nicely down the middle.

"Are you hiring a hall then," she asked, disingenuously.

"No need," said Graham airily, seeing a chance to impress her with his wealth and property once again. "If you open up the connecting door between the sitting room and the dining room, the place is as big as a bloody tennis court. Then there's the conservatory…but there won't be that many people, and she's not even getting a caterer in. God! All this fuss for some Northern tart and her brat! Cath should have stayed up there with them."

"She went to see them?" Mandy asked sharply. "You didn't tell me she went to see them!"

"Oh, she got some bee in her bonnet. I think she may have an inkling of our little arrangement." He drawled sleazily.

Mandy stood up and began to clear the table. If Graham's wife had some idea that this was more than a fling, then all her plans would be ruined.

"When do they arrive?" Mandy enquired, wanting to protect her investment.

Graham looked lazily at his Rolex. "About an hour ago." He smiled, looking forward to an evening of illicit bliss, but was cruelly knocked out of his fantasy by Mandy whipping his coat from the settee and handing it to him.

"Well, what the hell are you doing here?" she snapped. "If she finds out you'll ruin everything."

"But Mandy," he begged.

"Just go, Graham, and I don't expect to see you until Monday at work!"

He leant forward to kiss her.

"Go! Now! And be nice to your wife!"

He snatched his jacket from her and slammed the door as he left. If she felt Graham should play the perfect husband, well, he would, but there had better be a payoff from Mandy.

Mandy inspected her acrylic nail, damaged by Graham as he pulled his Jacket from her hand. "You'll pay for that, Graham," she muttered. "Oh yes you will!"

*****

Simon and Laura sat on the big leather sofa, Nicky curled sleepily on Simon's lap with his legs splayed across Laura's, Deefer the dog sleeping soundly on his lap. John looked at them and laughed.

"I hope none of you wants to get up too soon!" He chuckled.

"You've worn them both out, Dad," said Catherine.

"Nonsense!" said John. "They are just gathering their resources for the next onslaught! Quick, give me a sherry!"

Catherine laughed as she passed him the drink. "Anyone else?" The others all waved their hands in refusal.

"Helen?" asked Catherine, offering her the decanter.

"No thanks, Mum," said Helen, unusually quiet. "Where's Dad?" As she spoke Graham's key turned in the lock.

"Talk of the devil," John whispered, so as not to wake the sleeping child. As Graham entered the room he bellowed, "Hello, all!"

John nodded tersely, Simon and Laura went to stand up, Deefer jumped to the floor barking wildly, and Nicky began to wail loudly.

Within half an hour John and his guests were on their way to the cottage. Helen had gone to unpack in her room, and Catherine was pulling things out of the freezer to defrost for the next day's party. Graham had seated himself in the armchair, oblivious to the effect of his entrance on the gathering. With Catherine safely in the kitchen, he dialled his mobile. Mandy answered almost immediately.

"What?" she hissed.

"I'm all alone," he whispered. "Want to meet and pick up where we left off?"

Her response was as shocking to him as it was unexpected.

"Are you stupid?" she frowned. "I told you to make an effort to be pleasant to your family and I do not want to see you or hear from you until Monday."

"Yes, but…"

"I don't know what you are finding so difficult, Graham."

"But I want to see you!"

"I do not want to see you, Graham, until Monday. Do you understand?"

"Yes."

"I don't think you do, Graham."

"I do understand," he protested.

"Then tell me."

"You don't want to see me..."

"Or hear you!"

"Or hear from me, until Monday."

"That's right. Until Monday. Is that clear, Graham?"

"Yes, Mandy."

She hung up. His head fell to his chest, defeated. Mandy replaced the telephone receiver, smiled with satisfaction and punched the air with a "YES!"

*****

Catherine picked up the telephone; it was Floss.

"How's it going?" her friend asked, "and be honest."

"Well, I think I've been a bit ambitious. I should have started preparing earlier, but it was all a bit short notice. I have thirty people here for supper in a few hours. It's only a buffet, but I've made it all from scratch, and there are still quite a few…"

"Don't go anywhere!" Floss said, "I'm on my way!"

Floss arrived with a cooler bag stuffed with home-made goodies from her own freezer.

"Made these for a rainy day!" She put her apron on. "Point me to the salad!"

Bee was conspicuous by her absence. Her 'best friend' was giving a party for her son's engagement, yet Bee was in the hairdressers, leafing through a fashion magazine. The party presented Bee with a problem. Both

Laura and Helen were young and beautiful. And Bee would have to try very hard to outshine them. She looked at herself as the hairdresser applied foils to her already bleached head. It was exhausting trying to maintain her standard of beauty. She felt a frisson of resentment at Rogers's apparent unconcern at her efforts. After all, it was all for him, everything. In fact, it was exhausting being Bee.

The party began slowly, family already there of course, then other guests arriving in little groups as the evening progressed. Floss passed out drinks, and even Helen helped to take coats and direct guests to the conservatory for a drink, before the celebratory meal began. Floss had been introduced to Helen, but the girl was quiet to the point of being surly, any attempts at conversation were shut down, so Floss gave up trying. Graham held court loudly in the sitting room, regaling the guests with his banter, particularly the female guests, and doing absolutely nothing to help in any way.

In the kitchen, Catherine put the finishing touches to everything before taking it through to the already groaning buffet table in the conservatory. She had smartened herself up for this special occasion but her plum silk dress was hidden by a floral apron that had seen better days and her carefully pinned hair had escaped from its pins. As she wiped her face with a tea towel, wiping off the last traces of her make up, Andrew appeared in the kitchen.

"Need any help?" he asked. She picked up a laden tray.

"Oh, yes please! Just this tray and the last two over there... and did you notice if everyone had drinks?"

Andrew took the tray from her.

"You shouldn't be doing this," he told her firmly. "Mother of the Groom! Now go out there and join your guests. I'll handle this."

She looked at him with thanks and dashed off towards the sitting room.

"Catherine! You might want to look in the mirror first."

She was mortified. "Oh! Do I look a sight?"

"I think you look beautiful, but you are still wearing your apron!"

She looked down and laughed as she removed the apron, brushed herself down and set off to join her guests.

Soon Andrew and Floss appeared with the rest of the trays, placed them on the table and joined Catherine as she chatted to Simon, Laura and John. Catherine was bursting with pride as she introduced her son to her friends. They chatted easily together until Graham, tiring of telling the same old stories, stalked up to their little group and pushed himself between Simon and Laura. He put his arm around their shoulders.

"Now then Catherine, we can't have you and your catering friends monopolising the happy couple now, can we?"

He pushed his tanned and manicured hand towards Andrew, his expression saying, "And you are?" As they shook hands he presented, in a hostile look without words, the same question to Floss. She introduced herself with an explanation.

"We have met. Catherine helps me out at weekends, Mr Chandler, at the antique fairs."

"Oh," said Graham, in an exaggerated understanding, "the burger bar woman! Oh, I see! Oh, pleased to meet you, again, I'm sure," he said, shaking hands as if she had an infection. He turned aside to Catherine and cursed. "Why are they here? Keep an eye on the silver!" He spotted the latest guests arriving.

"Bee darling, at last!" he hooted, and sped towards his former flame. Catherine looked embarrassed enough for all of them.

Across the room, squeezing herself into a corner, Helen tried not to be noticed. She watched as Bee made her grand entrance. Helen could not help admitting that Bee did look stunning. In a gold full length dress which seemed only to be held together at the waist. With her perfectly tanned skin, styled hair and flawless makeup, Bee put everyone else in the shade. And yet Roger's eyes were casting across the room to find Helen. Finally, they locked eyes. Helen looked away and Roger started to walk towards her.

"I'll have a glass of champagne, Roger," demanded Bee, calling him back to reality. By the time he returned with her drink, Helen was with a crowd of Simon's old school friends, with whom she stayed for the rest of the evening.

Catherine said goodbye to her father and Nicky, who had plans to walk the dog and share an extended bedtime story with the Grandad.

"Splendid evening, darling," he said to his daughter. "Congratulations."

"I was glad you could meet Floss and Andrew," Catherine said, "I'm becoming very fond of them both."

"Oh yes," said John, thoughtfully rubbing his chin.

"What is it, Dad?"

"There's something about that Andrew. I feel sure I've met him before... Can't place him, though."

"Something good or bad?" asked Catherine, worried.

"Oh no, not like that. I just can't quite work out why he should seem so familiar. Oh well," he said briskly, "It'll come back to me, no doubt." With that he grabbed Nicky's hand. "Come on, pal! Deefer dog is waiting for us!" They both jumped in the waiting taxi and headed for home.

Catherine was just waving them goodbye when she heard Bees voice.

"Who's the sprog?" It was Graham who replied.

"That's the kid. You know, Laura's."

"Oh! The fallen woman."

"That's the one. Who'd have thought the reverend Holy Joe would have shacked up with a prossie!" They guffawed, and he took her arm and they entered the dining room, where Graham's voice grew louder.

"Come on, Bee. I will introduce you." Warming to his theme, his voice grew to a crescendo.

"Ladies and Gentlemen!" He raised his glass. "To the happy couple!" The guests turned and raised their glasses.

Simon and Laura smiled self-consciously; Catherine beamed with glad surprise as Graham raised his own glass

"A one hundred percent genuine, bona fide Vicar and his tart!"

There was an embarrassed, collective gasp followed by mortified silence. Bee squealed with laughter as Graham led her off, arm-in-arm. Catherine trembled with shame at her husband and hurt for her dear son.

Without skipping a beat, Andrew raised his voice along with his glass. "On behalf of Catherine, mother of the groom," he announced, nodding at her, "it is my great privilege to welcome you all to this celebration of the engagement of Simon and Laura." There was a little ripple of relieved applause as Andrew continued, "Catherine has asked me to express her extreme pride in her son Simon, and in his bride to be Laura, who is already a beloved daughter to Catherine and sister to Helen."

Helen stepped forward and slipped her arm around Laura's waist in a gesture of loving support.

"In Laura, he has found a life companion who shares his values, his commitment to serving others, and his faith - there'll be no stopping them now!"

Everyone laughed.

"May God grant you both all of life's blessings, and love's joys." He raised his glass. "To Simon and Laura!"

"Simon and Laura!" Catherine looked with gratitude at Andrew, then turned her attention back to her guests, refilling glasses, and clearing plates. Floss joined her in the kitchen, laying a friendly arm on her hand. "Catherine, it's been a good party. Don't worry."

Catherine was still shaking with humiliation and rage. "It was," she said, "until Graham decided to put on his little show. I'm so glad Nicky wasn't here to see it!"

Floss could not disagree. "The man's a monster!" she declared. "You should throw him out!" Catherine shook her head. "Come on," said Floss, "let's just sort this place out and get the night over with."

Like a pair of whirlwinds, she and Catherine stacked plates, washed, cleaned and tidied as much as they could, without actually snatching glasses from the guests' hands.

Andrew and Helen stood guard on Simon and Laura, ensuring that Graham could do no more damage. Sadly, and despite their efforts to protect the couple, nothing could hide the apologetic glances of the guests as they crowded round, offering their heartfelt congratulations, reassuring them that Graham had only embarrassed himself.

As soon as he could, Simon spoke privately to Andrew, thanking him for what he had done. "Anyone would have done the same," said Andrew, "I just jumped in first."

Andrew's speech had helped to restore the equilibrium temporarily, but the awkwardness lingered. The happy couple were far from happy, and after a few tortuous minutes of polite, half-heard pleasantries, and far sooner than expected, their guests began to make their excuses and leave.

"Mum," said Simon as they gathered in the kitchen, "would it be rude if we left now? We've got a long journey tomorrow."

"Aren't you staying for lunch tomorrow?" asked Catherine.

"Sorry, Mum. We have to leave early. You understand…"

Sadly, Catherine understood too well. The fact was, though it was only an hour since Graham's spiteful toast, the only people remaining were the family, Andrew and Floss. Even Roger and Bee had left, Bee more reluctantly than Roger, who seemed to be almost dragging her away.

Floss and Andrew appeared from the lounge where he had been vacuuming and she straightening up the cushions.

"We will be on our way now," Floss said, hugging Catherine. "Thank you for inviting us." She took Catherine's face in her hands. "You remember what I said."

The party was all over. Catherine stacked the last few plates into the dishwasher and began to wipe down the kitchen surfaces. Helen appeared at the door.

"Here, Mum, let me help." She pulled the broom from its cupboard and began to sweep the floor.

"That ended up OK, considering," Helen said.

"Considering how much your father had to drink, you mean."

"Well, yes. I was on a knife edge." Helen smiled. "You never know what Dad's going to say next, do you?"

"I have a pretty good idea, most of the time," replied Catherine.

Helen froze at Catherine's unexpected reply.

"You mean..."

"Helen, I have finally realised who I have been living with all these years."

"Mum! You know?"

"Yes, but I don't blame him, Helen. I really do blame myself. I have allowed him to get away with it, and," she crossed the kitchen and put her hands upon Helen's shoulders, "I want to tell you how sorry I am for making you put up with it all these years."

"Mum, what are you talking about?"

"Helen, I know watching me allow him to behave this way as you were growing up... it's made you... well..."

Helen understood. "Hard, cold... Is that what you mean?"

"Oh, Helen, I'm so sorry!"

It was Helen's turn to be the comforter this time.

"Mum, you couldn't be more wrong. Yes, I saw the way he treated you... us, in fact. But it just made me determined to take care of myself, to get away from him and never to let myself be held back by other people. To do it on my own. Mum, what are you going to do?"

"Well, I can't change your Dad, Helen. So..."

With that, and right on cue, Graham lurched through the door.

"Can't change me, eh? So what are you going to do? Lose a stone or three?" He laughed loudly and looked at Helen as his usual partner in these exchanges. "Eh, Helen?"

"Oh Dad!" Helen said, shaking her head. He stared at her, not understanding. He snatched the whisky bottle and a glass from the table.

"Well, goodnight girlies!" he shouted, as he lumbered up the stairs.

They both stared after him and in unison muttered, "Pinhead!" Then both giggled at their audacity. Catherine grabbed a half-finished bottle of wine and offered it to Helen.

"Actually, Mum I'd love a cup of tea. I'll make it. You sit down."

Catherine sat at the kitchen table and watched her daughter. Such a simple task, yet even that made her beautiful.

"No tea bags, Mum. Are the spares up the top as usual?"

There was something about Helen lately, something softer, gentler. The flowing lines of her party dress emphasised her tiny, fragile figure. Then Catherine noticed the fuller curve of her daughters bust, and, as she stretched up to reach the unopened box of tea bags, the material of the dress stretched across an unmistakeable curve. In sudden realisation, Catherine's hands went to her mouth. Her eyes filled with tears. Helen finished her task and turned to her mother, a mug in each hand.

"Ah, you can't beat a cup of…Mum! What is it?"

Helen sat opposite her Mother, putting the steaming mugs on the table in front of them. Catherine was speechless. She looked into her daughter's eyes as tears rolled down her cheeks.

"Mum?"

"Oh Helen, did you think you could do this all on your own? She indicated Helen's stomach." At once Helen began to cry. Catherine leapt from her seat, knelt beside Helen and held her close as her daughter sobbed, and sobbed.

*****

Sunday morning early, Catherine drove to her father's house to try to persuade them all to come back with her for lunch. She was surprised to find that it was Laura who was most insistent that they should return home as soon as they could. Catherine had always thought it best to 'suck it up' to save any embarrassment. She had spent her whole married life swallowing her pride and pain so that Graham would not be hurt. Laura, on the other hand, said she would only ignore what had been said for Catherine's and her father's sake, but she would go no further.

"If I ever see him again, it will be to ask for an explanation for what he said, Catherine."

Simon looked like a man convinced from experience that Laura meant exactly what she said.

"Dad?" pleaded Catherine.

"No, I am eating here, Catherine. That man has gone too far this time. You can't carry on as if nothing has happened."

Defeated, Catherine returned home. After an enormous Sunday lunch, it was time for Helen to go. The taxi was at the door. As she opened the passenger door, Helen's eyes searched out her mother's.

"Love you, Mum," she said. The taxi drove away and everyone returned to the house. Catherine was just straightening everything up when there was a knock on the back door. Roger peeped around the door. "Just wondered if Helen wanted a lift?" he asked brightly.

"Oh Roger, there must be some confusion. Helen left just now, and she took the train."

Roger was lingering there in the door way. "Oh, I see. Well…"

Catherine really wanted to get on with straightening up the house after the busy weekend, but Roger seemed in no hurry to go. "I was just going to make a coffee. Would you like one?"

Roger accepted with enthusiasm. As Catherine heated the milk, Roger just sat there in, it seemed, a nervous silence.

"Is there something on your mind, Roger?"

Roger opened his mouth to speak, and as he did Bee came slamming through the door.

"Oh, there you are. What are you two at then, having a secret meeting?"

"Coffee?" offered Catherine.

"Thanks," said Bee, accepting the cup Catherine had just made for herself. Catherine sat at the table and waited, she no longer felt she had to fill the silence and, as neither of these two had been invited in, she felt it was up to them to make conversation. Bee was the first to speak.

"Glad to see the back of that noisy little brat, I bet."

"Do you mean Nicky?" Catherine asked. "I think he's adorable, an instant grandson, and Dad has already got him learning chess!"

"Shouldn't he be at school instead of swanning around with his single mother?

"It's half-term, Bee." Catherine closed her down, but since Bee had already tired of the subject, which had no relevance to her, she switched to her favourite activity, tearing other women to shreds. But since both Laura and Helen were dear to Catherine's heart, Bee was not having much success in that area either. Her attempts to ridicule Laura's poor dress sense fell on unreceptive ground, so she turned to Helen.

"I did think Helen looked a bit peaky, Catherine. Is she okay?

Roger looked up from his contemplation of the skin on his coffee.

"Just tired, I think," Catherine answered. "She works so hard, you know."

"Oh yes," nodded Bee, with a glint in her eyes, "I expect that's it. Doesn't look quite as glamorous as she used to, though, and she's put on a bit of weight, I noticed. Must be all those motorway take-aways! She is definitely looking heavier, don't you think, Roger?"

Roger blinked as if he was processing something very slowly and carefully through every part of his mind.

"You really should tell her to be careful, Catherine, after all, the family does incline towards obesity." She looked pointedly at Catherine, trying to belabour a very obvious point.

Roger spoke. "You were skinny when you married Graham, weren't you Catherine?"

Catherine was taken aback at such a bald question.

"Well, yes," she answered, "but then…"

Bee was surprised but delighted at Roger's sudden shift to her point of view. She took the opportunity to push her advantage.

"But then what, Cath? Too many cakes and full-fat coffees, eh?"

Catherine blushed. "Actually, I never really lost the weight after I had the twins…"

Bee drew in her breath to spit another unkind remark but did not have the opportunity. Roger stood up suddenly, his chair falling and crashing to the tiled floor.

"God help me!" He cried. "I am a stupid, stupid fool!!"

Catherine and Bee looked at him in stunned surprise as he almost ran from the kitchen, leaving the door open behind him. The two women looked at each other, then, as the sounds of Roger's car starting up reached them, Bee jumped up and rushed out, swearing and shouting as he drove out and away. Had she known he was driving away from her for the last time, she may have been a little more upset.

Fourteen

Monday morning, and Catherine had just finished her usual telephone call to her father, who had just got off the phone from Nicky. It seemed the boy was doing a school project on the Romans and absolutely had to ask 'the grandad' what he knew. John suspected that Nicky thought he had first-hand experience of riding in a chariot and wearing a toga. Father and daughter laughed together and arranged to meet later in the week.

Catherine replaced the phone in its cradle and it rang almost as she set it down. Having ascertained that she really was Catherine Chandler, the caller identified herself as the lead on the Echo New Writers Competition. Catherine had won and her first article would be in this week's edition of the Echo. In a state of shock, Catherine agreed to meet with the editor and sponsor at the Echo office that afternoon. Catherine returned to the kitchen, poured herself a large sherry, and sat down

*****

Helen was coping with the morning sickness now. She had found that a slow start and, surprisingly, a large breakfast, helped. She smiled to herself as she remembered last night. She had been in the bath, half asleep and tearful, as she had often been lately. Then came a crazy knocking on the door. She heard her name called by an unmistakeable voice.

"Helen! Helen! It's me! Roger!"

Without thinking she wrapped herself in her terry robe and padded to the door, opening it only as far as the safety chain would let her. Roger saw her confused face.

"Helen, I know, I know, and I'm so happy! Look!" She realised he had armfuls of bags and packages and a huge Eeyore under his arm.

"Look!" he said again, diving into one of the bags and pulling out a tiny pair of socks. Then from another bag a white sailor suit, then a lemon hat with bunny ears, then a succession of outfits for every occasion from new born to age three.

"You'd better come in," Helen said, opening the door and crossing to the sofa. She sat down, then, leaning forward, picked up one of the stuffed bags. "What else have you got in here?" she laughed, pulling out a tiny football kit, complete with boots.

*****

As Catherine left the editor's office, having signed the necessary forms and posed for the necessary photographs, she noticed a missed call on her mobile, from Floss. Sitting in the car, she returned the call.

"Hello, Floss," chirped Catherine, as the call was picked up.

"It's me, actually," Andrew replied.

"Oh, er, ah...hello," Catherine stammered, immediately wishing she had said something a little more intelligent. "Is everything okay?"

"Not really. Well, nothing serious, but Floss has turned her ankle, so she won't be able to do the antiques market on Wednesday. She is just ringing round to cancel, but she wanted me to call you first."

Catherine thought fast. It was the run up to Christmas and one of their busiest times. "No, don't cancel," she said, "I have an idea!"

*****

For the first time in a very long time, both Helen and Roger were very late for work. So late, in fact, that they didn't go in at all. Helen looked at him. They were on the floor, surrounded by baby clothes and determination.

"Are you absolutely sure?" she said to him.

"Sure, I'm sure," he said.

Suddenly she sat up and looked at her watch. "Oh my!"

He looked at her. "What is it?"

"My ante-natal appointment. I have a scan in an hour! Come on!!"

*****

Catherine arrived at Floss' cottage and set about making her comfortable. They spent the rest of the evening together and Catherine convinced Floss that she was perfectly capable of running Milady's Snacks for the day on Wednesday; and by Saturday Floss should be up to the job herself, provided she followed her doctor's advice and rested her ankle completely until then. Catherine promised to return the following day and to stay overnight so that she could make the necessary early start on Wednesday morning. Catherine headed for home, forming her request to Graham for an 'overnight pass' as she drove.

*****

Laura and Simon hardly spoke on their journey back North. Simon was ashamed of his father, and Laura was just ashamed. She acted angry but the truth was, she was hurt. Graham may have been drunk, but his words were a little too close to the mark to be ignored. After a very long time, with Nicky fast asleep on the back seat, she spoke.

"Simon, if you have changed your mind, I will understand..."

Simon pulled the car to a halt, leaned over and kissed her. "Don't be daft," he said. "I'd marry you tomorrow if I could."

*****

Roger needed to sit down. The scan had been wonderful, life changing, and, at the moment he saw the picture, Roger knew he had chosen life with Helen above everything else.

"It won't be that easy, Roger," Helen whispered as they leaned into one another. "I am sure your awful wedded wife will not give you up without a fight."

"Ah! That!" said Roger.

"Hmm, yes. That!"

"Well...the thing is...Bee and I...well...we are not actually married!

Helen hugged him with delight. The plans they had made, the dreams they had, a small home, a simple life, a family business. Yes, they were still possible. Even more possible now. The future loomed ahead full of possibility, full of joy, full of... Helen leaned back from the hug, and looked into his eyes. They whispered in unison, "Twins!"

*****

Graham was surprisingly accommodating when told of Catherine's plan to stay Tuesday night with Floss and work the whole of the next day at the antiques market. He even suggested she stay longer. Not convinced or perplexed by this less than typical show of understanding, once Graham had left for work on Tuesday morning, Catherine packed her overnight bag, her laptop, and set off for Floss' house.

Graham planned to impress the unimpressible Mandy with his home and the promise it held. He even went so far as to pop into the florists at lunchtime, a thing he had never done during the whole of his married life and ordered a dozen roses to be delivered to Mandy's desk later that day. The note read simply 'Meet me!'

*****

"Mum has guessed about the pregnancy," Helen told her brother, "but she doesn't know who the father is, yet." She glanced across at Roger and squeezed the hand she was holding. The three of them had arranged to meet at a garden centre café where they were most likely to remain anonymous.

"I know it's a bit of a shock," confessed Roger, "I have acted despicably towards Bee, I know. I should have come clean long ago. I have stayed with her

224

through laziness, not love or even loyalty. But she does not deserve this."

They talked and talked. The decision was made, Roger would be honest with Bee, and the plans Helen and Roger had made for their future would follow.

Helen hugged her brother closely and arranged to see him and Laura soon.

*****

Floss had dozed off. Her painkillers had the added advantage of knocking the patient out cold for a couple of hours, so Catherine set up her laptop and opened her emails.

Nothing worth noting in 'focused', she clicked on 'other' and there she saw 'Kirsty Jordan-Hughes @dailymonitor.com.' Opening the email, which was from the Sunday editor of the popular national newspaper 'The Monitor.' It seemed their chief editor had been sent her articles by the editor of the Echo and would like Catherine to call at her earliest convenience to discuss her contributing a series of six 'Agony Aunt' columns in the New Year, with a view to extending if the articles proved to be popular.

She had told no one yet of her competition win and this unexpected outcome had her flummoxed. Could it actually be true, was she actually good enough to write for a national newspaper? Floss awoke just as Catherine sent her response, promising to telephone the next day and positively sparkling with resolve.

*****

It began to dawn on Bee that she had heard nothing from Roger in two days. His phone was turned off, and when she called his company, they said he was sick. His sudden departure after the conversation with Catherine was bewildering but offered no explanations as to Roger's failure to call her. Strangely, Bee had no fear for his safety or no real feelings of concern. She was merely peeved that he was absent without leave. Roger had had sulks before, even tried to leave once. But she had merely redoubled her efforts, appealed to his dutiful nature and they had eventually slotted back into their usual rut. Strange though, that he had left with nothing but his wallet, his passport and his car...

*****

Mandy and Graham 'bumped into each other' at the door to the building as they left. "Would you like a lift to the railway station, Mandy," Graham asked loudly, for the benefit of anyone who would listen. Mandy rolled her eyes and stomped ahead of him to the car park where she got into his car with one fluid movement. Graham got in beside her.

He began, "The ball and chain is away for the night…"

"That's no way to refer to the woman in your life, Mr Chandler!" Mandy teased.

"You are the woman in my life, Mandy," he purred, playing right into her hands as always.

"I suppose you want to show me where you live then. A bit of illicit rumpy-pumpy in the marital bed. Is that it?"

"Well, I hadn't thought as far as that," Graham answered, "but now you mention it," he licked his lips lasciviously, "that would be a really, really…"

"Well, let's go then!" she ordered, and Graham complied.

*****

Catherine answered Floss' door. It was Andrew. He had come to take his sister-in-law and her friend to dinner. Floss insisted she could not come and the other two, naturally, protested that she must. However, as always, Floss had her way and Catherine was comfortably seated in the front of the Range Rover, as Andrew drove her to a local pub that had a fast-growing reputation for excellent food. From the start, they fell into easy conversation. Catherine, without the constraining presence of Graham, was a witty and informed dinner partner. She had no need to impress, no fear of humiliation. Unlike Saturdays with the usual crew, the cringe factor was at zero. Catherine began to feel that she could truly relax. She took a deep, satisfied breath, savouring the moment.

"Everything alright?" Andrew asked, looking at her with concern.

"Oh yes!" Catherine smiled. "I was just trying to identify a feeling… do you know I think I might actually be… happy!"

As the meal came to an end and they enjoyed their coffee, Catherine confided in Andrew about her new job. He was, of course, thrilled for her, and curious as to the subject of her articles.

"You'll just have to wait and see…if it gets that far," said Catherine.

As they left the pub, the sky was clear and the ground was frosty. "It's going to be a cold one," said Andrew. "They're predicting snow tomorrow."

Catherine was horrified. "I can't believe I didn't think of bringing a warm coat for tomorrow!" she exclaimed.

"You can borrow one from Floss."

"Well, if I don't want to button it up, or move my arms, I'll be okay," laughed Catherine, "but thanks for the offer. Don't worry. I'll be fine," she said brightly, trying to convince herself as much as her companion.

Unconvinced, Andrew suggested they drive back to Floss' house via Catherine's, so she could pick up her coat and gloves. It was agreed that this was an eminently good idea and off they went. Pulling into her drive, Catherine realised that only the bedroom lights were on.

"Oh," she said, "I think Graham is home after all.

"I'll wait in the car," said Andrew.

As Catherine unlocked the door, the unmistakeable sounds of noisy adultery floated down the stairs. Catherine felt at once angry, wretched and ashamed. She crept up the stairs and pushed the bedroom door open.

At that moment, all those feelings seemed to drain into the floor. At the ridiculous picture of her husband in the act of betrayal and of his scheming young mistress in the act of…well, acting, Catherine found she felt only amused contempt.

The flawless, blank-faced but very vocal young woman noticed her first. Her expression moved from aloof disinterest to genuine shock in a split second.

"What the hell are you doing here?" she enquired of Catherine, as if she were asking directions at a supermarket.

Graham froze, perplexed. He turned his head, following Mandy's cold gaze.

"Catherine!"

The pair sat up against the headboard. Graham pulled the bed cover up to his neck as he positioned himself side by side with his lover. The girl, Catherine noted, did not cover herself. Rather, she stretched her arms above her head in an act of defiant contempt, all the time keeping her eyes locked on Catherine's.

"Are you finished, Graham?" Catherine asked, "because I would like you both to get out of here as soon as possible."

The two lovers looked at her; he like a rabbit caught in headlights; she looking far more like the cat that had got the cream. In fact, she licked her lips.

With that, Catherine's composure cracked. "Get out!" she screamed. "Get out now!" she stepped towards the bed side, grabbed the under sheet and pulled, tipping the pair in a scramble of arms and legs onto the floor.

Graham stood first, grabbing his clothes and running down the stairs. Mandy, believing that a strategic retreat at this point would be the best option, grabbed the duvet and ran down the stairs, pausing briefly to pick up her handbag and phone from the dressing table. They both ran out into the frozen night.

Andrew had been musing on the very pleasant evening he had just spent and was just got to wondering why Catherine was taking so long when the most extraordinary, surreal scene took place in front of him. The door opened and, instead of Catherine, out ran Graham and, presumably, his mistress. She was wrapped in a bulky duvet and he was clutching a bundle of clothing to his groin, whilst desperately trying to open the door to his car, parked on the gravel driveway.

"Hurry up!" she shrieked. "I'm freezing!"

"I don't have the…" As he spoke a bunch of keys flew through the air from the doorway, hit the bonnet of the vehicle and landed on the gravel. The sight of the naked Graham on all fours in the darkness, groping through the gravel for his keys was pure comic indecency. Just as Andrew thought his laughter would give him away, Graham found the keys and, with a shout of triumph, opened the car. Both jumped in, slammed the door, and the car sped away, leaving only a crumpled duvet and one black sock in their wake. Realising what had happened; Andrew went into the house, to find Catherine sitting on the stairs, shaking with laughter.

*****

The next day, customers of Milady's Snacks found Catherine efficient and friendly as usual, if a little distracted. Catherine was indeed distracted as her mind was processing the events of the previous night. Following Graham's undignified exit, Andrew watched as timid, compliant Catherine became fierce determined and decisive. Her laughter had briefly turned to tears and just as quickly, she took a deep breath, stood up and said, "Right, let's get this mess tidied up."

First, Catherine called an emergency locksmith and paid an exorbitant fee to have every lock in the house changed that night. While they waited, both Catherine and Andrew bundled all Graham's belongings into bin bags, everything, every item of clothing, gadgetry and the even the ludicrous pile of grooming products taking up most of the space in the bathroom. She stripped the bed, rolling the sheets, the duvet and the adultery into one big wad of garbage and squashed it all into the last bin bag. Finally, she called a taxi, filled it with the black sacks and paid the driver to deliver it all to Graham's office first thing in the morning.

Andrew drove her back to Floss, who was filled with pity and admiration, pity that Catherine should be confronted with such a graphic demonstration of her husband's treachery and admiration for her boldness and resolve.

They both urged her to forego tomorrows 'Milady' duties, but Catherine would not hear of it. And so it was that she was wiping down the tables after the lunchtime rush as someone tapped her on the shoulder. Catherine was startled and turned swiftly to see Bee, garishly adorned in heavy 'natural look' cosmetics and wearing a mauve faux fur coat.

Bee wore her usual smirk, Catherine offered her a menu. "Coffee or tea?" she asked.

"Neither from here, thank you," retorted Bee.

Catherine looked around for Roger, or one of Bee's car driving golf buddies. She noticed that Bee was not carrying her usual pile of purchases; it dawned on Catherine that Bee was only here for one reason.

"How did you get here, Bee?" she smiled.

"I drove, of course. Roger is still AWOL and no one else…"

"Was available at such short notice?" Catherine finished her sentence, amused by Bee's obvious agenda.

"You are really taking the antiques business seriously then, Bee. I know you only drive yourself in extreme circumstances!" she laughed.

Bee may even have blushed under her carapace of foundation. "Well, yes," Bee answered, "now I think of it I *will* have a black coffee. Maybe you could join me?"

Catherine walked the short distance back to the van, as Bee teetered along behind her. She entered the van and shut the door behind her, forcing Bee to take up the position of an ordinary customer, standing at the raised counter with Catherine at some height above her. Catherine passed her the coffee across the counter swiftly, as Bee took some coins from her purse. "It's on the house," said Catherine, and began to serve another customer, then another.

She took her time, seeing that Bee was hanging around, itching to ask about the events of the previous night. As the last customer walked away with his cappuccino, Catherine turned to Bee. "Was there anything else?"

Bee shook her head. "Not really," she paused, "but now you come to mention it, I was just checking to make sure everything was okay."

Catherine looked her square in the face. "*I* certainly am, why do you ask?"

"Well, I couldn't help hearing a bit of a commotion last night at your place and when I went over this morning the house was all locked up"

"That's right," said Catherine, giving her no clue and no quarter. She turned to slap several large rashers of bacon on the hot plate for her next customer.

Bee, seeing she would have no opportunity to gloat or gossip, attacked further. "There's no need to be rude, Catherine. I was only trying to help a friend," she whined, "and this is the thanks I get!"

Catherine, rosy cheeked and resplendent in her striped pinafore and spotty headscarf, glared down at her self-styled friend. Suddenly the large spatula in her hand looked more like a weapon than a cooking implement as she pointed it at Bee.

"No, Bee, if you wanted to help, you would have told me years ago that my husband was a serial adulterer." She put her hand up in a firm 'stop' as Bee opened her mouth to speak. "And if you really wanted to help," her fingers formed quotation marks, "as a friend..." Bee stepped back as if pushed, and noticed a little crowd had gathered to watch, as Catherine continued, "If you really wanted to help, you would not have slept with my husband in the first place. Now, get out of my sight, I have a job to do here."

The crowd applauded. Bee turned on her designer heel and jostled her way through the crowd amidst shouts of, "Well said, Cath!" "You told that tart, Mrs!" and "Shame on you, old floosy!" and a few more ribald observations on her morals.

Bee drove home, defeated. She had hoped for a bit of scandal and it turned out *she* was the scandal in the eyes of all the market folk. Driving in her fancy little car down the motorway, she considered Catherine's words. Even more, she remembered what the people in the crowd had called her. This time she did not brush them off in a self-important huff, those words *hurt*. To Bee, appearance was everything, but it had begun to dawn on her that if she were to reach her hands beneath the surface of her perfect home, her perfect life, her perfect body and her perfect face, she would find they held absolutely nothing.

After packing up and returning the van, Catherine drove slowly home. She was pleasantly tired from a day's hard work, but the scene with Bee had threatened to lift the lid off her tightly controlled emotions. It is not every woman who could come home and find her husband in the act of adultery, then go to work the next day as if nothing had happened.

As she let herself in, the house felt still and polluted. Catherine wandered through each of the rooms downstairs, remembering happy times and sad. For the first time, it occurred to her that Graham had been mostly absent, and only occasionally, grudgingly, present for most of the important events in their family life. Catherine reached the kitchen, put her 'Milady' uniform in the washing machine, and walked naked up the stairs to shower the smell of cooking from her hair and body. She stepped into their bedroom to use the en suite. The bed was stripped to the bare mattress, Graham's wardrobe and nightstand open and empty. She slipped off her wedding ring and laid it on the now bare mattress; as she left the room, she closed the door behind her and walked to the family bathroom along the landing.

Standing under the hot jets of water, Catherine finally allowed herself to cry.

Soon afterwards, Catherine, in her cosy pyjamas and dressing gown was flicking through the TV channels, trying to avoid all the cheery 'happy family' Christmas adverts. Her mind on overdrive, switching from enormous remorse to enormous relief, she tried to plan ahead. Quiet tears seemed to leak from her eyes uncontrollably. Exhausted, she collapsed onto her knees and wept.

Her phone buzzed a text from her father:
"The Lord is close to the broken-hearted and saves those who are crushed in spirit."
Psalm 34:18.

He did not normally discuss his faith with her, since Graham had expressly forbidden any such talk in their house. So, for John to text her scripture boldly was remarkable. Catherine phoned her father back.

"Thanks for the text, Dad, it's perfect."

"I'm glad you like it, he answered. "Wasn't too sure whether or not to send it"

"Coincidentally, Laura gave me a card with the exact same bible verse on it!"

He laughed, "I'd say it was more than a coincidence. So, how are you doing?"

Her voice cracked, went a little high pitched. "Dad I'm not doing too well, to be honest"

He started putting his coat on as he spoke. "Sit tight, I'm on my way."

He arrived a short time later, and, walking into the lounge, noticed an open Bible on the table beside his daughter's chair. She saw him glance at it.

"I haven't undergone a sudden conversion, Dad, I just wanted to see the rest of the Psalm," she said. "I dug out my old Bible, look." She pointed him to the inscription at the front.

'To Dear Catherine on your 16th Birthday, with Love from Mum and Dad. "The LORD bless you and keep you; the LORD make his face shine on you and be gracious to you; the LORD turn his

face toward you and give you peace."
Numbers 6:24.

"That's your mum's writing," said John, sitting on the arm of her chair. "She would be so pleased to see you read that! Your mum never stopped praying for you. Never. And when things looked bad between you and Graham, that was her hope for you, that you would find peace. It was not long after that things started to unravel a bit…"

Catherine looked at him and saw him for the first time as person in his own right. A man who had nursed his wife through several bouts of illness, with little support from his only daughter who was prevented from doing more by a husband who mistreated and deceived her. "Oh Dad," she said softly, "I'm so sorry for everything!"

He hugged her, "It's all in the past now, forgotten and forgiven, if there was ever anything to forgive."

"I'm glad Graham is gone," she said. Catherine mopped her eyes with her sleeve, and put her head in her hands.

"Dad," she whispered, "have I done the right thing?"

He put his arm around her shoulders and squeezed, "Absolutely, definitely the right thing my girl!" he said firmly. "That man has abused you for the last twenty-odd years, Catherine. The decision you have made, it's overwhelming, it's daunting, but it's spot on. Good riddance to him!"

He jumped up, grabbing her hand. "Come on," he said, "this is no time for tears, it's a time for celebration. I've got a bottle of bubbly stashed away for Christmas! You can stay at my place and I'll drive you back in the morning.

Within fifteen minutes Catherine threw some clothes in an overnight bag, secured the house and jumped in the car, still in her pyjamas.

Fifteen

Bee slept soundly as a letter popped through the brass letterbox and landed softly on the Italian tiles of the porch. She still had not heard from Roger, and following yesterday's debacle at the antiques fair, she had needed more than a few large Gins to reclaim her equilibrium.

Several hours after the letter arrived, Bee completed her lengthy beauty routine, dressed in her high fashion sports outfit and headed to her garage. She noticed Catherine's car was not on the driveway and inwardly grumbled that she had better get used to driving herself everywhere, since Catherine obviously was holding a grudge nowadays.

She almost stepped over the letter, until she recognised Roger's handwriting in the address. Perplexed, she picked it up and carried it with her to the car.

"Why couldn't he just phone?" She grumbled, as she opened the envelope, trying hard not to damage her nails. The words on the card could have been in Swahili for all Bee's understanding of them. She had to read them again. This time, the language became clear.

"WHAT?" She shouted, reading the note for a third and final time.

She threw her head back against the headrest, stamped her feet and let out a sound somewhere between a roar and a scream. Then, throwing the note on the passenger seat beside her, she shut her door, pulled on her seatbelt and drove to the gym. The note drifted into the foot well, face up:

> Dear Bee,
> I am grateful for everything, but now it's over. You can keep everything. I never wanted any of it, after all.
> So sorry,
> Roger

*****

Simon and Laura had been huddled in the church office with the Reverend for nearly an hour. Despite her efforts, Pearl could hear nothing through the door as she slowly and unnecessarily polished the door frame.

"Pearl!!" shouted June, vigorously waving her arm to shoo her sister away from the door. As Pearl left her 'dusting,' June, leaning on the still-buzzing vacuum cleaner, reminded her that listening at doors was considered rude.

"I couldn't hear anything anyway - you need to turn the hoover off," advised Pearl. June laughed and did just that.

The door opened and a very happy Simon and Laura almost skipped out of the office. The two ladies looked for information to the Reverend Tim, who poked his head round the highly polished door frame and simply said, "You're doing a marvellous job, the place looks smashing!"

Pearl, straightforward as ever, could not contain her curiosity any longer. "Simon!" she called. The couple stopped and looked back at her. "What's going on?" She put her hands in the air in a dramatic gesture.

The pair looked at each-other and then at Pearl. In joyful unison they shouted, "We're getting married!"

*****

As Simon was signing the papers and planning the first official steps towards marriage, Catherine was taking the same steps to end hers. The solicitor advised her that being eyewitness to Graham's most recent adultery, their subsequent separation, along with lack of any substantial property or dependent children meant that the divorce could be cut and dried in less than a year. Catherine completed all the paperwork then and there. From the solicitors, she went to the bank and opened an account for herself, transferring exactly half of the balance into her account. It wasn't an enormous amount and they had no savings, since Graham's lust for vulgar ostentation meant they had spent his monthly cheque before it landed in their joint account. She then withdrew a few hundred pounds in cash from the ATM and set off for home.

*****

Simon had gone to find Bill, who was working at a large luxury hotel in the run up to Christmas. His lunch break was coming up shortly and Simon was keen to tell Bill of the upcoming wedding before he heard it from anyone else. Of course, Bill was overjoyed, and they toasted the good news with a hefty mug of hot chocolate. Knowing that Bill normally had the third weekend of the month off, Simon said he would see Bill on Saturday. A shadow crossed Bill's face, "Not this weekend," he said. "It's my mum's birthday, remember?"

"You're going back to that place, even after what happened there?"

"Well, it's not mum's fault, and I don't want her to think I've forgotten her," he said decidedly.

"Would it be okay if I came with you this time?" asked the gentle young man beside him. "I have something important I need your help with, and we could talk about it during the drive down."

Bill did not object, initially because he wanted to know what the 'something important' was, but mostly because he dreaded seeing the fearsome Deirdre and her crew again.

Saturday morning saw them take the drive to the neat little cemetery. Simon laid a little bunch of flowers beside the headstone and stepped away to allow Bill, kneeling beside his mother's burial place, some time alone. After a short interval, Bill stood, bowed, and nodded. Simon joined him.

At that moment a commanding contralto boomed across the graveyard. "I say, hullooo, is that you Bill?"

They turned and saw a large woman in church vestments standing in the entrance to the Church. Bill looked at her in terror and then back at Simon, grabbing his arm. "RUN!" he cried. And they did, with Deirdre in hot pursuit.

Back in the car, racing along the motorway, the two of them laughed until the tears rolled down their cheeks.

"Now," said Bill, "one good turn deserves another, Vicar. What was it you need my help with?"

A short time later, the bridegroom and his newly appointed best man, arrived back at St Christopher's in time for the 'plan the wedding' tea that June had set up.

They were all seated around the table which was groaning with piles of Pearl's delicious cakes, and a selection of sandwiches and savouries. Nicky, seated on Pearl's lap, was drawing an elaborate picture of a Christmas tree, with all his hoped-for gifts underneath it.

Bill's position as Best Man had been loudly applauded, and now the Reverend Tim was calculating the wedding date. "Well, you need a minimum of twenty-nin days between getting the license and getting married. By my calculations, the earliest you can get married is…" he ran his hand across the calendar in front of him "Christmas Eve!!"

They all hooted with joy, repeating "Christmas Eve!" in various tones of excitement.

Laura, ever the voice of reason raised her hand and everyone fell silent. "I don't want to be a party pooper," she said, "but won't everyone have made Christmas arrangements by now? It's bit much to ask them to change everything for us."

Everyone looked downcast.

"Hold on," Simon responded, "where were you all going to be this Christmas?"

Every one of them, of course, had no other place to be than at Christmas than St Christopher's. It was soon established that the people most important to Simon and Laura, these friends, her parents, his mother, sister, and grandfather could just as easily have Christmas at St Christopher's than 'way down south with no snow,' as Pearl so aptly expressed it. Simon and Bill could stay with the Reverend Tim and his wife on the eve of the wedding; his mother, sister and grandfather could stay in Simon's flat. Laura's parents had already planned to spend Christmas with her, and beyond that, neither of them could think of anyone else they would miss.

It was agreed, the plan set in place, and all that remained was to tell their families the good news.

Laura stood up. "There is one more thing I would like to say," she said. They fell silent "Well, two things, really. Simon has his best man, and I would be very honoured if you June, and you Pearl, would be my Maids of Honour."

Applause followed this suggestion and Pearl was already wondering if a tiara would be too much, when Laura came to her second request. "Go on mummy!" encouraged Nicky.

"It's your idea Nicky, you go ahead," Laura nodded to him.

Nicky swung round on Pearl's lap. And put his arms on her shoulders. "Will you make the wedding cake, Pearlie?" he asked.

*****

Catherine had picked up some of her father's favourite marmalade in town and made a detour to his place on her way home. Catherine first related her day's achievements, then they settled into the usual comfortable chat over tea, toast and marmalade. The house phone rang.

"It's Simon," he declared, looking at the display. "I wonder what he wants at this time of day?

"Just answer the phone, Dad," she laughed.

John picked up the receiver. Catherine could not quite hear the other end of the conversation, and her father wasn't giving much away. He seemed to go rather pink and Catherine began to wonder if he was okay. She was just about to reach for the phone, when he said, "Well, yes, yes, I understand, thank you very much." And hung up the phone. "Well I never!" he declared, grinning from ear to ear. "Fancy that!"

The suspense was killing her. "What's going on, Dad?"

"Our boy is getting married on Christmas Eve!"

It was another hour before Catherine finally left to go home, followed by a long, happy phone call with Simon and Laura. She was under strict instructions to keep the wedding to herself; it was strictly family they said, and that did not include his father.

"You didn't have any plans this Christmas, did you mum?" asked Simon, in his excitement he had just assumed his mother and grandfather would be spending a quiet day together with Helen.

"Nothing I can't cancel," she said. "Grandad and I had booked to have Christmas dinner with Floss and Andrew at the Angel Inn, that fancy place in town. I will sort it out tomorrow."

"Oh, mum, I'm sorry. You must have been looking forward to that, and I know how much you enjoy Floss' company."

Catherine would have liked to add that she was not averse to Andrew's company these days either, but thought better of it. She heard Laura in the background saying, "Why not invite them too? They were so kind to us at that awful party."

It was arranged. Catherine was to break the news to Floss and her brother that their Christmas celebrations were now to include a long drive, an overnight stay, and a wedding.

She slept in Helen's bed that night, a long, peaceful sleep.

Sixteen

When Graham turned up at her flat after the embarrassment of all his belongings arriving at work, much to the amusement of the whole building, Mandy was tempted to turn him away. Still, she felt the situation might be salvageable. After all, he had a massive salary and a massive house and he was not too awful looking. They lay in bed; Mandy certainly knew the easiest way to a man's heart, and his bank balance. Graham leaned across her. She noticed how the skin hung from his face in folds as he looked down at her.

"I love you, Mandy," he whined. "I want to be with you forever."

"Well, we can't both live here forever," she replied. "How soon do you think things will be sorted out?"

"How do you mean?" he said.

"The divorce, the settlement, the division of property, etcetera!" she snapped impatiently. "A year? Two?"

He looked at her blankly.

"All your worldly goods?" she asked.

As he looked at her, the penny began to drop. "All my worldly goods are stuffed into my company car outside your flat," he protested.

"No, Graham," she insisted, "the house, the savings, whatever! Your half, after the divorce!"

"Oh, that!" Graham muttered.

Graham discovered that Mandy had no intention of allowing Graham to hop conveniently from his home to hers. On the contrary, he was expected to leave his comfortable home and comfortable wife and make an honest woman of his mistress. Somehow the reality of the situation hit him like a cold shower.

He sat up on the edge of the bed and braced his shoulders. His 'angry pose' usually did the trick with these girls. He waited for her to twine herself around him in passionate apology. He waited. And he waited.

Mandy looked on, quietly applied a slick of lip gloss and fluffed out her hair on the pillow, pulled the duvet down slightly to reveal a hint of her naked body underneath. She smiled to herself as Graham sighed and flexed his back once more, then, as he turned, she closed her eyes and settled her lips into an inviting pout. He was angry, the sight of her albeit beautiful self, sleeping peacefully while he, the victim of the piece, was in torment. It was too much to bear.

"How can you sleep, Mandy. I am in *torment! My life is falling apart!*

She opened her eyes, lazily.

"Firstly Graham, don't be such a drama queen and secondly, *don't ever* speak to me in that way again."

He looked at her. "I will speak as I please," he bellowed. Then, deciding it would be more effective to play the hurt lover, he dropped his hands to his side and looked away from her once again. "Oh! You just can't understand…"

"No, Graham. *You* don't understand."

She slid gracefully from the bed and wrapped herself in a silky dressing gown. Her tone was calm and firm.

"I want you to leave now, Graham." She walked around to his side of the bed, gathered his clothes up from the floor where he had left them. "Come on!" she said. "Up you get!"

Confused, he stood.

"Start walking!"

Graham reached for his clothes as she walked him to the door and managed to grab his boxers, struggling to put them on as he walked.

"Mandy you have to understand. I'm upset!"

"No, Graham," she said firmly, as they stood at her front door. "*You* have to understand. You are not to use that tone with me. Ever. Do *you* understand?"

With that she put his bundle of clothes in his hand along with his keys and wallet, and in one fluid movement, pushed him gently through the door onto the pavement. She shut and locked the door and turned out the light. Graham was indignant and shocked at finding himself half-naked on the street for the second time in 24 hours.

*****

Bee worked extra hard at the gym, trying to thrust away the truth. Inside her she screamed in anger. How dare he? She stamped her foot. After all she had done for him. After all she had achieved for him, sacrificed for him, what was there to show for it? She showered, changed and drove home, the little note shouting at her from the floor of the car.

Catherine was in, she noticed, but still no Graham. Either he was becoming very brazen in his infidelity or Catherine had finally ditched him.

Bee stood in her tastefully designed hallway. She remembered little note, ending years of dedication and hard work on her part. "…you can keep everything, I never wanted any of it."

She looked around and thought "I can keep everything? Everything?" It did not sound so bad, after all.

Bee surveyed 'everything.' A collection of rooms, each one exquisitely fitted out in its own perfect style. Her eye fell on the usual pile of interior design magazines, and she idly flicked through one of them. She sat back, leaning into her vintage Gropius chair and closed her eyes. The beginning of a tear began to slide from beneath her eyelids and then, try as hard as she could, the tears just wouldn't stop. She cried for the years she had given to Roger, the unwilling 'project' on whom she had set all her care and the depths of her love. And in the end, he had just walked away from it all.

"I never wanted any of it, after all."

And where was he now? Everything left with her!

"I never wanted any of it, after all."

And she had known.

She had known he did not want it, but she had ploughed ahead all the same. Seeing his potential, just as she had seen the potential in this run-down old house and restored it, restyled it, reshaped it, to a set of rooms that could grace any of her glossy magazines. She became hideously aware that she had never loved Roger, only the idea of what she could make of him. In that moment she let him go.

"What can I do now?" She asked herself. "What am I? WHO am I?"

Without something or someone to improve, Bee was lost. Then, pouring a glass of wine, she sat alone as the room grew dark and the moon lit up the world around her. Suddenly she took a deep breath and stood.

"I can take something plain and make it outstanding and unique. I turn coal dust into diamonds!" she said to the moon. "ALL BY MYSELF!"

*****

Friday morning came, and Catherine had gone out early to look for a wedding outfit, although Simon and Laura said it was to be a very simple affair, she just could not let the day go by without marking it with clothes for such a special occasion. She found a beautiful matching coat and dress and couldn't resist purchasing a couple of toys for Nicky, her nearly grandson. It would be wonderful to spend Christmas with a child again. Returning to the car, she phoned Maurice the hairdresser, who made space for her as near to the big day as possible.

As Catherine opened the front door, carrying her shopping bags, she had to step over a fat brown envelope on the carpet just inside the door. The phone machine was blinking with a message. Catherine dumped her purchases on the table, taking care to hang the matching dress and coat on the door before she pressed the play button.

"Hello, Catherine. This is Kirsty Jordan-Hughes from the Monitor Newspaper Group. I am ringing to let you know that your article will be published in this Sunday's 'Me' magazine, the supplement to the Monitor on Sunday. I have sent you a contract through the post and would be glad if you would have it looked over, then sign and return it as soon as possible. Please call us as soon as you get this message."

Catherine snatched up the contract. The newspaper was offering her a very respectable sum for her weekly articles; she would be financially independent, but above all, she was actually to be paid for doing something she loved - definitely time for a cup of tea!

*****

Bee was not one to feel sorry for herself. In fact, she didn't have the capacity to feel sorry for anyone. It seemed incomprehensible to her that Roger should give up all he had on a whim. Her answer to Roger's letter was to visit the salon, top up her tan, and try to figure what to do next. "I have everything!" she kept telling herself.

Just as Catherine sat down with her cup of tea, Bee hurried unceremoniously through the door, and seated herself at the table. Catherine hurriedly slid the contract into her apron pocket and made Bee a coffee.

"What's up?" she asked

"Roger has left me," Bee announced flatly.

"What!" Catherine was dumbfounded.

"I know," Bee said. "Shocking isn't it?"

Catherine looked at her. She had changed.

"You don't look very..."

"Upset, devastated?" Bee finished her sentence. "No. Strangely, I am not as distraught as I thought I would be."

"Oh, Catherine," Bee said softly, putting her hand on her friend's, "I have been awful, haven't I? I'm so sorry."

Catherine took in her perfect face, careful makeup, not a hair out of place. The same Bee, but not the same Bee.

"Catherine, you have always been a good friend to me, and I have been…a…a brat!"

Catherine laughed, "No, Bee…"

"No, Catherine, I mean it. I don't think I've ever really been happy with Roger. He was never unkind to me… he was just so *boring*. Well, I don't think I ever really loved him, just the idea of him. I took it out on everyone around me, including him."

Catherine was alarmed at this sudden stripping back of Bee's self-deception. It was so very unexpected and hard to deal with. What ever would she say next?

"Catherine, I…Graham and I…Well, it was a few years back, I was wrong to fall for..."

Catherine held her hand up to stop her before things got out of hand. "Bee! Stop! I know, and I don't want to know any more. Bee, Graham is gone...for good. I hope and you and I are still friends and neighbours. Let's keep it that way."

"Not for much longer," Bee said.

Catherine looked disconcerted.

"Neighbours, that is. I hope we can still be friends, in spite of everything."

Catherine assured her they would of course remain friends. Bee confided that she needed to sell the house and rid herself of the enormous mortgage. Indeed, she wanted to get away from the scene of her folly and make a fresh start, somewhere new.

"You know, Catherine, I have finally realised that if I can do all this for Roger," she waved her arm in the direction of her soon-to-be-former home, "then I can do it for me. Just me. On my own."

Catherine saw her, determined, almost excited, and, at last, grown up.

"You know, Bee," she said, "I really think you can!"

*****

So close to Christmas, all Graham's work colleagues and golf club friends found there was absolutely no room at the inn for Graham. He paid for a week at a 2-star B and B, after his ignominious rejection from Mandy's flat; and after much searching and a ridiculously large deposit he moved into a tiny, dirty, studio flat that the previous tenant had left in a hurry. Graham had found himself alone with only his ego and about thirty bulging black sacks for company.

At work he maintained his bluster and assured Mandy it would not be long until he got his rightful share of everything.

He was not unduly shocked when an application for divorce was served to him at work just a week before Christmas, although the supporting statement for adultery was very specific and very descriptive.

Seventeen

Roger and Helen drove to Lancashire a couple of days before the wedding, where they would be staying in Simon's spare room. Helen dozed in the passenger seat, her hand resting on her belly. Roger smiled. This, he had finally discovered, was all he had ever wanted.

Catherine, John, Floss, and Andrew all travelled up to the wedding together on the 23rd. They had booked a hotel, "A bit of Christmas luxury," Floss had said. Frankly the thought of everyone squeezing into Simon's tiny flat was preposterous, and Helen was quite happy to have the place to herself, she told her mother.

That evening they had an early dinner at the hotel, and Catherine was delighted to find that her father and Andrew hit it off in a big way, although why that should be so important to her was a mystery. They found a great deal to talk about and although John had said more than once that he was sure they had met before, Andrew insisted they had not.

Catherine had been told that all she needed to do was to turn up at the church at eleven o'clock. Everything else was organised. John had to get there earlier and told Catherine that he had been asked to help organise things. Arriving at the church with Floss and

Andrew, Catherine was pleased to see the place full to bursting with Simon's friends and it seemed half the town was there to celebrate the wedding. The church itself was glowing with thousands of fairy lights, adorned with festive garlands and a perfect specimen of the traditional English church at Christmas.

Bill, the Best Man and unofficial Steward, showed Catherine to her seat, then took his place beside Simon at the front. Reverend Tim, standing in his customary spot, looked out across the packed church. He nodded and smiled broadly at Catherine, in the second row back, since the front pew was reserved for the maids of honour. Catherine smiled back, wondering where on earth her father was. Andrew and Floss stood beside her; Laura's mother smiled from the corresponding pew across the aisle. The fact that Simon and Laura had specifically excluded Graham was sad, but not unexpected. Catherine was surprised and pleased to see Roger seated across the aisle, although he had chosen to sit in the reserved pew in front of Laura's mother. Maybe he was taking photos. She waved, and Roger waved back, nervously it seemed to her. She was just becoming irritated at her father for being so late when the wedding march began, and the congregation stood to attention.

Everyone turned to look as Laura's father entered, his beloved daughter at his side. Laura wore a sparkling lace gown and veil, and carried a bouquet of red roses and gypsophila. As she stepped along the Victorian tiles to stand beside her Groom, Nicky followed behind, smart and serious in his red and gold waistcoat, bearing the rings on a red velvet cushion. June and Pearl came in next, resplendent in Christmas coloured tulle, with Poinsettia bouquets and sparkling tiaras.

Helen's father placed her hand in Simon's and stepped back.

There was a lull as they all took their places and the organ began to play again. Catherine and the rest of the congregation turned, some more surprised than others to hear a second wedding march. Helen, on her grandfather's arm, processed down the aisle, wearing white and carrying a bouquet to match the bride's.

"She looks more like a bride than a bridesmaid!" Catherine thought.

Catherine reached forward to lovingly pat Nicky's shoulder, but froze in mid-action. Roger was no longer in his seat, but standing beside Simon and Laura

John placed Helen's hand in Roger's and stepped back. Roger looked down at Helen and kissed her cheek.

Catherine, astonished, swayed and sat down with a bump. She laughed, then cried, then laughed again. In a flash, it all made sense. The long absences, the recent 'kindly' lifts from Roger, the sudden departure of Roger when he realised Helen was carrying his child. That Roger was her son-in-law would take some getting used to, and the fall-out for Bee did not bear thinking about.

But Helen had never looked happier, nor Roger more in love.

The congregation buzzed with excited curiosity at the sight of Catherine weeping with joy and laughing in shock. Helen looked across at her with a radiant smile, on impulse she dashed across to her mother and hugged her. "Is it a *nice* surprise, mum?"

Catherine hugged her back "The best surprise" she replied, "Now go and get wed!"

The Reverend Tim began: "Friends, we are gathered here together to witness," he turned to Simon and Laura, "the joining of this man and this woman," then to Roger and Helen, "and this man, and this woman…in Holy Matrimony…"

Catherine wondered if she would be able to concentrate on the ceremony at all but of course, she savoured every moment of it, and cried through most of it, beaming from start to finish.

As the wedding party and their guests gathered in the hall for the reception, they were greeted by tables piled high with all types of festive food, lovingly prepared by the St Christopher's House 'family.' The hall was decorated in the most Christmassy of Christmas charm, the ceiling festooned with handmade paperchains and the tree heavy with lights and baubles. Spectacular though this was, it was agreed by all that the most outstanding piece of all was, without a doubt, the multi-coloured, three-tiered cake, in the shape of a star.

After the meal was over and the dancing had not quite begun, Catherine was taking a few moments by herself to recover, when John appeared with a large mug of tea.

"Here you are, dear," he soothed. "Strong and sweet, just what you need for shock." Catherine had had something a little stronger in mind, but tea would just have to do it for now.

"Oh," said her father, "talking of surprises, I think I remember how I know your Andrew."

"Dad! He's not my Andrew, he…"

As they spoke, the man himself appeared, with Floss at his side. "Did I hear my name mentioned?" he asked.

"Yes," she replied. "Dad was just about to tell me where he remembers you from."

She missed the almost imperceptible shake of the head and raised eyebrows, as Andrew signalled to John his wish to keep their connection secret for a little longer. John looked puzzled but complied.

"Well, Dad?"

"Do you know, it's gone again, dear…senior moment!" Just then, the band struck up a tune and the newly married took to the floor, to a hearty clapping from the assembled guests, who couple by couple, joined the dance.

Floss, placing her hand on John's shoulder, said

"Oh, I would *love* to dance, John, thank you so much," and propelled her somewhat surprised partner into the crowd.

Andrew looked down at Catherine.

"Have you recovered?" he asked her, tenderly.

"Just about," she assured him.

Catherine looked at her father and her friend, waltzing around the dance floor, chatting busily and throwing the occasional conspiratorial glance in her direction.

"I don't know what those two have got to talk about so intently," she declared, impatiently.

"Oh, I have a pretty good idea," Andrew said, moving even nearer to her.

"They are definitely talking about us" she said, looking up, suddenly aware of his closeness.

"Let's give them something to talk about then," he said as he took her hand, "Shall we?"

*****

The following morning, Helen and Roger, Laura and Simon, along with Laura's parents, all came to the hotel for breakfast, before saying their farewells. It had an almost formal feel, and Catherine was not surprised when Simon rose to his feet to shouts of, "Speech! Speech!" from the assembled party.

"Good morning to you all," he said. "Now I've got your attention, I do have something to say."

Having got through all the preliminary thanks to everyone assembled, and praise of his bride, Simon surprised and delighted them all by saying that he and his new family were moving to the South. Simon and Laura had been offered a job at the charity headquarters, St Christopher's House, in London.

"So, you'll all be seeing a lot more of us," he smiled, "once we have found somewhere to live!"

Amidst cheers and more congratulations, he took his seat once more. John and Catherine looked at each other. Each knew what the other was thinking and both smiled. Simon and Laura would be living in the house Simon had grown up in.

By late morning the car was packed up and they were on their way down the motorway. Catherine reached in her handbag and drew out an envelope.

"What's that?" asked Floss.

"Helen gave it to me; told me not to open it until I was sitting down. I guess now is as good a time as any!"

Catherine read through the letter than sat back, stunned.

"What is it?" asked Floss. "What's happened?"

Catherine passed her the letter. "Read it out, please."

Floss read:

"Dearest Mum. Firstly, I want to thank you for always loving me and caring for me, however badly I behaved towards you. I don't think I ever really understood how you could do that until I became a mother myself. Secondly, I want to explain about Roger. It did start as a silly affair but, Mum, for the last year I have known that Roger and I are deeply in love. We are committed to establishing a secure and loving home for each other and for our children. And I am as sure as I can be that he and I, and the twins, will be as happy as any family could be. Love you so much, Mum. Helen xx."

Floss looked at Catherine, still unmoving in her seat. "Twins!" was all she could whisper. "I'm going to be the grandmother of twins!"

They all chatted happily on the journey home. Somehow, after a break for coffee, Catherine ended up at the front, seated next to Andrew, who was driving. Floss and John dozed, noisily, in the back. She and Andrew spoke easily of recent events. She felt she had known him for years, but that this handsome, gentle man could actually be interested in her as more than the friend of his sister had never occurred to her until this weekend.

Thoughts of Catherine had, however, occupied Andrew's mind almost constantly since he had first met her. She was so unlike anyone else he had met, and he found her extremely beautiful, although she would never believe it to be so. The best made plans, so they say, are laid long. And Andrew had very definite plans for Catherine.

As they swung into the approach to Floss' house, Andrew called out, "Wakey! Wakey!" and both John and Floss snorted themselves awake. Catherine was confused when they drove past Floss' Gate House home and continued into the estate itself.

"Where are you going?" she asked Andrew, who had a look of deep concentration on his face.

"Short detour," he said.

Eventually, they pulled up outside the huge pillared entrance to Parlstone Hall. Catherine looked at Andrew, then at Floss and John, all of whom were smiling broadly. The great oak door opened and a very respectable looking, liveried butler appeared.

"Good afternoon, My Lord, My Lady." He bowed to Andrew, then to Floss. "The drawing room is prepared."

Catherine was struck dumb, and followed mutely as they all tripped into the great hall itself. Seated in the drawing room, it was explained that Andrew was in fact, Lord Andrew Starling-Sprake, Duke of St. Peverill, Earl of Parlstone and Hansworthy, keeper of Parlstone Hall, the family estate and the town house in London, only brother of Floss' late husband.

Catherine looked at Floss. "So 'Milady's Snacks'…"

"'Fraid so," admitted Floss.

It was John who had blown their cover, recognising in Andrew the profile of his late brother, with whom John had served for a short spell in the Guards.

"But why couldn't you just tell me?" asked Catherine.

"Things can get so *complicated* when people know," said Floss. "Some people can't see past the title and the property."

Catherine looked slightly put out.

"I don't mean to be offensive," Floss continued, "and I don't mean you personally, but there are those who…"

"I understand," Catherine agreed. "Really, I understand." She thought of Bee and Graham. How obsequious they would have become. She cringed and shuddered openly, then laughed out loud.

"What is it?" asked Andrew.

"I have *got* to be there when Graham finds out!"

*****

Finally, in her own home, in Helen's bed, Catherine fell asleep. It seemed she had only been asleep for five minutes, when she was jolted awake by the ringing of her telephone. That, and her mobile, were both blasting away in chorus. She grabbed the house phone first.

"Yes?" she asked, wearily.

"Mum!" It was Simon. "Have you seen the Monitor? You're in the papers. Go get the papers, mum!"

She sat up in bed. "Oh!" Just then her mobile began to ring again. "I have to go. My mobile's going off!"

It was Helen. "Have you seen the papers?"

The house phone started ringing again, then the doorbell. She ran downstairs to answer the persistently ringing front door.

"Dad!" she cried, as he rushed through the door carrying several identical copies of the Sunday Monitor, a bottle of champagne and two glasses.

"You're in print, Katie mine. You've done it!"

Catherine looked down at the magazine. There, next to her photo and her maiden name, Katie Dean, was her first article.

Epilogue

Following Graham's many adulteries, a fast-track divorce was granted on the grounds that there were no dependent children and no assets or property involved in the settlement. The 'no assets or property part' was of great surprise to Mandy, who found herself out of love with Mr. Chandler without his wealth, as quickly as she had loved him with it. His employers, sensitive to Grahams increasingly sleazy reputation, moved him to a small office on the industrial estate and sent him on a training course entitled 'Developing Appropriate Behaviour in the Workplace.' Graham found himself alone in his studio flat, an aging lothario with a flagging career and a dodgy reputation. He was never quite the same man again.

Bee sold up 'everything,' and bought herself a flat above the shop in a rather nice part of Cheshire. The shop is very successful, and her style of design is particularly popular with footballers and their wives. The shop's name is 'Beatrice Interiors' - pronounced in the Italian style.

Roger and Helen and the twins settled in a small semi-detached house, outside Birmingham. She continues to run the salon, and Roger runs his own design company from home, whilst caring for the twins.

Simon and Laura very quickly settled into the home that he had grown up in and would inherit, and within the year, Nicky became a proud big brother to baby Katie. 'The Grandad' is a very frequent visitor to the family.

Catherine's writing career, of course, developed. She built on her journalistic success with a self-help book, 'Never too late,' which is fast becoming an international bestseller.

To no-one's surprise, Catherine and Andrew announced their engagement at Katie's christening and it was no more than a year before their marriage was announced in the Monitor, the Times and the Daily Telegraph.

Blank page

Faith, Hope & Christmas Trees

Faith, a veteran radio journalist famed for exposing scandal, has a long buried secret of her own. Hope, her office cleaner, has four children, three jobs, dependent in-laws and an exhausted husband.

Two women who should never have met are thrown together when Faith reluctantly agrees to cover Applebury Christmas Tree festival. In this tiny English town, a run-down garden centre, a dilapidated church, and a cast of unexpected characters are transformed as the Festival approaches.

Finally, when Faith's hidden past is cruelly laid bare her future is changed for better and for ever. 'Faith, Hope and Christmas Trees' is an inspirational story of courage, forgiveness, hope and healing for the festive season.

Blank page